The Guns of Ellsworth

The Guns of Ellsworth

by Dwight Bennett

DOUBLEDAY & COMPANY, INC.

GARDEN CITY, NEW YORK

1973

All of the characters in this book are fictitious
and any resemblance to actual persons,
living or dead, is purely coincidental.

ISBN: 0-385-08352-1
Library of Congress Catalog Card Number 72–92234
Copyright © 1973 by Dwight Bennett Newton
All Rights Reserved
Printed in the United States of America
First Edition

The Guns of Ellsworth

CHAPTER I

The tiny house must have been white, at one time, before fierce Kansas summers checked and blistered the paint and Kansas winters scoured it down to the raw timber. Within, the furnishings looked shabby enough to Vern Balance as he halted on the doorstep, letting the screen door close against his heel. There was a pungent smell of medicines, and a murmur of voices beyond an inner doorway; crossing to this he could see the seated figure of a man with graying sidewhiskers and, on the edge of a chair facing him, the shoeless kid in the frayed overalls.

It seemed to be a matter of a hurt foot. Eyes solemn on unshed tears, the boy flinched and squirmed as the deep cut was swabbed with iodine. "Hold still!" the doctor told him sternly, and shot Balance an impatient look. "You'll have to wait a few minutes. Got a little business with broken glass, here."

"No hurry," Balance said. "Mine's more or less a social call." Keen blue eyes probed at him a moment from behind heavy lenses; then the man returned to his work, and Vern Balance strode restlessly back through the waiting room and out again upon the porch.

As everywhere else in the village, a stillness lay here that was broken only by a hot rush of wind in cottonwood branches overhead, the swaying creak of the shingle with its legend: HOWARD RADLEY, M.D. July's heat lay like a physical weight. A few geraniums, growing in tin cans set along the porch railing, made the one spot of color against the drabness of the dusty street.

At last the screen door opened and the doctor emerged, a hand resting on the youngster's shoulder. "Now, Jimmy," he said, "next time you go to jump fences, you be careful where you land. Hear?"

"Yes, Doc." And Jimmy was gone, limping painfully on the bandaged foot. Rolling down his shirt sleeves, the little doctor shook his head. "Not a chance, naturally, of getting shoes on them at that age . . ." He cocked a glance at the waiting visitor, then.

"All right, Vern," he said gruffly. "Let's step inside."

That got a look of surprise, as Balance let himself be ushered back into the house. "Doc, I was beginning to think you didn't remember me."

"You've changed some," the other admitted. "But it's only natural. That place can do it to a man."

"*You* look about the same."

Radley shrugged. "Well, and how long has it been? A couple of years. Seems longer to you, I guess."

"More like twenty."

"Yes . . . Well, sit down—sit down. Let me pour you a drink."

He was already heading for a bottle and glasses on the sideboard when his guest stopped him. "Not for me, Doc. If you don't mind."

It earned him a quick look over the tops of gold-framed spectacles. "You get out of the habit while you were in there?"

"Not exactly. Sort of a promise I made myself. I haven't had a drink since that night."

The doctor studied him a moment longer. "I see." Nodding, he left the bottle where it was. "Yeah, you've changed . . . How about coffee, then?" he suggested. "I think I got some made."

"Coffee would be fine."

Over his shoulder, as he started for the door to the back of the house, Radley said, "I suppose you've looked around town. Maybe you've noticed a few changes, yourself."

"It's not even the same town," Vern Balance agreed. He had dropped his bowler on the round center table but he remained standing—a tall young man, gray-eyed and blunt-featured, showing the rebellious urges that pushed at him. "I just dropped off the westbound, an hour ago. Took a walk along Texas Street and couldn't believe it. Everything closed and boarded up: the Bull's Head—even the Alamo standing empty and gutted, with its windows broken . . ."

"Well, it's sure not the Abilene *you* knew." Radley spoke from the kitchen, where there was a busy sound of cabinet doors being opened and closed. Now he returned with an enameled coffeepot in one hand, a pair of china cups dangling from the bent forefinger of the other. He set the cups on the table and poured, and steam rose from the swirling dark liquid. "Of course," he went on, "things were bound to change after the farmers got muscle enough on the city council to have the quarantine laws enforced, and the Texas drovers ordered elsewhere with their beef."

"Haven't the farmers cut their own throats?"

Howard Radley shrugged. "Sugar? Milk?" As the other shook his head to both suggestions he went on, "It did look, at first, as though Abilene was surely done for. Still, we've managed, with more and more grangers coming in to fill up the prairie round about, where the longhorns used to graze." The doctor dropped with a sigh into a sagging armchair, where he tested the temperature of the coffee in his cup by sipping it gingerly. "Of course, the pace is slower now. A number of our merchants who traded mostly with the Texas outfits have pulled stakes and followed the rails, sixty miles west to Ellsworth. Did you see what happened to the Drovers Cottage?"

"I saw where it used to be." Balance made a face over the strong, reheated brew. "Looked like nothing left but one wing, and the foundation. Did it burn out?"

"A year ago this spring, Jim Gore picked up his hotel and moved it to Ellsworth in one piece—all but that rear wing. Just put it on flatcars and hauled it off! Well, it seems to be the general opinion that Ellsworth has got the Texas trade cornered, for the time being anyway. Though I've heard it's pretty slow everywhere, this summer."

Not commenting on that, Balance said, "I notice *you* haven't gone yet."

"And I'm not budging." To prove it, Doc Radley eased himself down more comfortably in the sprung-bottomed chair. "A man in my line of work has too busy a time of it, in a cattle-trail town. I found that out, here in Abilene. I'm getting to the age where I like things better, now that it's quieted."

"But can a man of your ability really be satisfied with delivering babies and doctoring the colic—and maybe bandaging up cut feet?"

"Suits me fine. I'll let some younger fellow get rich, patching bullet holes at all hours of the day or night.

"Enough beating around the bush," the doctor added abruptly. "What about you? You're out, and I'm glad—though somehow it never occurred to me I'd be seeing you back in Abilene. They give you a bad time in there?"

Balance shrugged. "It could have been worse. Especially since I figured I got no more than I had coming."

"Glad you can see it like that." Radley slanted an upward glance at the man standing by the table—the spare but well-built frame, the gray eyes in the clean-shaven face. "You're fined down some; whatever work they had you on must have done you good. And looking at you, I doubt anyone would guess you'd just walked out of prison."

"If you mean the suit, it's two years old. Train fare took most of what money I had."

"Hmm. Got any plans?"

"Why, I go with the tide," Vern Balance told him. "Like all the rest, I'm on my way to Ellsworth."

"Ellsworth!" The doctor's head jerked. Appalled, he reached to set his cup, unfinished, on the table. "You don't mean to tell me you're going right back into that—?"

Balance interrupted. "It's not what you're thinking, Doc. I was a damned fool, in those days. I've put all that behind me—the cards, too. What I *will* do next, I really don't know; but it happens I've got some unfinished business and Ellsworth is where I have to go to settle it. A man that owes me money—I need it, and I mean to try and collect."

"It might not be all you'll collect! Have you stopped to consider, Clayt Spearman's more than likely to show up in that town before the summer's over? Or some of his crew, at the very least."

"Am I supposed to let that keep me away?" the younger man retorted. "I've got no quarrel with Clayt Spearman. God knows I'd give anything to undo what happened two years ago—but, nobody can do that. The boy's dead; there's no way to bring him back. And meanwhile I've stood my trial, and served my time."

For a moment, as neither spoke, the quiet came in and enveloped them—the wash of wind in the trees outside, the ticking of a clock on the wall, the rhythmic squeal of a distant pump handle that ran on awhile and then ceased. The doctor rose and paced a few steps. Halting he said, "I've often wondered if you really understood that trial of yours. It was pure politics—Civil War politics, at that. Had it been held before a Texas jury, instead of here in the Dickinson County Courthouse, Clayt would have seen you hang. Acquitting you of murder for killing his son was the jury's way of telling him he couldn't run Kansas law, too."

"It wasn't murder!" Vern Balance insisted, as he set his own cup down. "The court understood that. It was just one of those stupid card-table killings. I kept winning, and Bud Spearman kept getting hotter under the collar—but I was feeling too good, from the stuff I'd been drinking, to care. When that second spade king showed up in my hand, *he* was the one started the shooting. I only defended myself. I just did too good a job of it."

"Of course—of course. And you were lucky the jury believed your character witnesses, when we tried to tell them you weren't the kind to deal out of your sleeve . . . So they made it manslaughter, and gave you two years—and that was politics, too: It was a first step in serving notice that Abilene was fed up and ripe for a general house-cleaning—to get rid of the Texas trade, and the saloons and the gambling and the killings, and everything else that went with it. You just happened to be available, as an example and a warning.

"Then, just a few weeks after they took you off to Lansing, that Hickok fellow brought things to a head. Did you hear about that?"

Balance nodded. "I heard some reports, in prison. I don't doubt they were garbled."

"What happened was, he staged a killing spree—went after his personal enemies while wearing the marshal's badge. Gunned down Phil Coe, who you remember was Ben Thompson's partner in the Bull's Head, and ended by killing one of his own deputies by mistake . . . Mike Williams, a local fellow everybody liked. There were plenty of people here in Abilene who'd never thought much of a killer like Wild Bill Hickok as their town marshal, but were afraid to cross him. What happened that night gave them their chance to get him fired, and then go ahead and serve notice on the Texas trade.

"And so it moved to Ellsworth—and if you don't mind my saying so, I still think that's the one place you should stay away from."

"Sorry, I can't oblige you. I told you: I've got business."

The doctor swore softly. He walked to an open window and scowled at the blast of shimmering sunlight. He ran a palm across white beard stubble, shook his head. When he turned back, a question was reflected in his eyes. "And if you do run into Clayt Spearman? He's a proud and vindictive man, and losing his son was a bitter blow to him. Do you honestly think you can avoid trouble with him?"

"I don't intend to be in that town much longer than overnight, if I can help it," Balance told him. "I certainly won't be looking for trouble, but I can't spend my life running away from it—or from Spearman, either. I know how to look out for myself and I mean to be left alone!"

"I see . . ." Radley shook his head, studying him narrowly through his thick lenses. "You *have* changed. A couple of years ago you were a footloose, likable young fellow who didn't have much idea where he was going, and maybe liked the liquor and the cards a shade too much for his own good. What's more, they ended up getting you into serious trouble. But still, you had a zest for things, that made you a pleasure to know . . ." The little man sighed. "I can't see that there's much of that young fellow left. You've matured, of course; but I also see somebody that's turned hard—and for that, I'm sorry."

"Killing a man, and serving time, can have their effect," Balance pointed out dryly.

"But go to Ellsworth now and you could wind up having to kill again!"

For a long moment the younger man met his disapproving stare. Slowly, then, he shook his head. "Sorry, Doc. Nobody appointed you my conscience! I'll always be grateful to you, standing up for me in court. But maybe coming to see you like this was a mistake. I'd not, had I thought I'd get a lecture. Now I guess it's time I was going." He took his hat from the table where he'd laid it.

The doctor lifted his hands and let them fall. "All right—no lecture. But you came to me for *something*. What was it?"

Balance had actually taken a stride toward the door; Radley's words turned him back. After a moment he said, "You read a man well, Doc! There *is* one thing you might be able to tell me: A girl I knew here, two years ago—Lucy Wagoner. You must remember her—her father ran a little pharmacy, north of the tracks in the better part of town. Today, I find the building's empty—no sign of anyone. What happened? They go to Ellsworth, too?"

The other man didn't answer at once. "I thought that might be it," he said finally. "Well, son, they've neither of them gone anywhere. Bert Wagoner's up on the hill; the cholera took him, over a year ago."

"I see. And—Lucy?"

Looking at him directly, Radley said, "Her name's Jenson, now. She married a farmer—a good, steady sort of chap. They've got a hundred and sixty acres, out north of town."

For a moment the stillness was so complete that the sound of insects snapping in dry weeds outside the open window came clearly in to them. "How far north?" Vern Balance asked finally.

"I don't think I'll tell you that. I can't believe it could do any good."

Howard Radley met the storm that beat up swiftly in that other pair of eyes; but it was over in an instant, and the younger man's lips thinned and the anger settled. He hesitated a moment longer, as though seeking something to say. Then, giving it up, he merely shrugged and turned again to the door.

The doctor followed him that far, calling, "Take care of yourself, boy." But after that he could only stand, helplessly scowling through the screen door as his visitor strode off along the boardwalk, in the swaying shadow of the cottonwoods.

CHAPTER II

Balance tramped the streets of Abilene, at loose ends, irritable and dissatisfied. Damn Howard Radley! He'd thought of the man as a friend, not an interfering busybody; and it made no difference, after all, that Doc had refused to answer his final question. This could not stop him. There were other ways of finding the Jenson farm for himself.

And after that?

Slowly and reluctantly, in the end he had to let what he had learned seep home. It was true, then—it was really true! A prop he'd allowed himself to hold onto, these two years, was gone; and hard as it was, he found he was already adjusting to it.

There had been nothing definite, after all—no promises, nothing more than a few clandestine meetings, against the threat of her father's wrath had he known; a few embraces. And then, after the catastrophe, nothing at all—no messages, not even a glimpse of her in the courtroom during his trial. Which, of course, wasn't to have been expected, either. Bert Wagoner would never have let her come there, least of all if he suspected his daughter had any personal interest in a gambler and adventurer, on trial for a killing over a saloon card table.

Vern Balance wondered suddenly if his attraction for her might not have been the element of danger she sensed, in someone so different from the village boys and farm lads she normally was thrown together with. But even for a romantic young girl, his actual conviction of manslaughter might have been just a little too much to accept.

He knew suddenly that Radley had been wiser than he. Yes, it was far better that he go away from here and never see her again . . .

And then he saw her.

She stepped from the doorway of a store, almost directly into his path, a bundle in the crook of one arm. She drew back and he watched recognition dawn. Blue eyes flew wide, the color drained from her cheeks; a hand lifted to her opened mouth.

The hand, Balance saw, wore a narrow gold band. It was roughened with work; her face, between the wings of her poke bonnet, had weathered and darkened and what he could see of her hair, that had burned like spun gold, now looked drab. She was no longer quite the pretty girl he remembered—a year of the hard life of a Kansas homesteader's woman was already beginning its work of turning her old.

"Hello, Lucy," he said.

He offered his hand but she did not appear even to see it. Her eyes remained on his face. She spoke his name tentatively, on a half breath, but it came out as a question—as though she still did not really believe what she saw. He said, "I'm glad to see you again. It's been a long time . . ."

"It seems long," she said faintly.

Then a man stepped out of the door, directly behind her, and from the look that crossed the fellow's face Balance knew at once who he was. In fact, he thought he remembered Lucy's husband as someone he might have seen around her father's pharmacy, those long months ago. He was a towhead, good-sized, with a shag of shiny yellow beard from not having used a razor in the last day or so. There was a cording of muscle on the forearms beneath the rolled sleeves of his hickory shirt.

It was very likely he had been hanging around the edges of Lucy's life, waiting to be noticed, at a time when all her interest had been in a more colorful rival. Now there was quick suspicion in his scowl and in his voice as he demanded, "Who's this stranger you're talking to?" He swung his head around belligerently and suddenly his cheeks began to redden. "By God!" he exclaimed.

Lucy tried. "Ted," she said in a shaken voice, "this is—"

"I see who it is!" he retorted. He stepped to put himself between them, and protuberant pale eyes glared his anger. His hands were drawn up into fists. "Jailbird!" he gritted. "Murderer! What for you come back here?"

"Shut up, Jenson!" Balance kept his voice level with an effort. "I got a right to go wherever I want."

"The hell you have! I see you tomcatting after my wife—right here in front of the town. By damn, I show you!" And suddenly one of those fists, hardened to hoe and plow handle, made a sweeping arc.

His move was clumsy, and Vern Balance had no trouble pulling his head aside. Two years on the rockpile had given Balance a respectable plating of muscle across his shoulders and upper arms; and his reaction had always been exceptionally quick. Now, as that craggy fist brushed past his ear he shot one hand up, seized the wrist and gave it a hard sideward jerk. Ted Jenson was caught off balance and his own weight, against the fulcrum of the captured arm, swung him around and slammed his shoulders hard against the jamb of the open door. Breath gusted from his open lips, and then Balance stepped in and brought his other forearm firmly across Jenson's throat.

Jenson grunted a curse and tried to break free, but he was pinned. Vern Balance, for his part, was almost oblivious to the man's struggles, or to the choking sounds that tried to escape from him. But at last he became aware of the girl pawing at him and her terror as she cried out her husband's name, over and over. With a shake of the head, like a man coming out of deep water, he shrugged her hands away and stepped back.

There was little fight left in Ted Jenson; when he'd been released he crouched against the store front, gasping for breath, and Balance told him coldly, "Understand this: A man can come to this town—if he'd have any reason to, any more—without wanting your wife. So quit fussing, mister. You'll neither of you be seeing me again!"

He looked at Lucy Jenson—pale, disheveled, her bundle lying at her feet, staring at him now with something very much like loathing—and he felt nothing at all; if anything, a kind of pity for what he could picture her becoming, in a few more years. Luckily there'd been no witnesses to the scene, and no one to interfere. Without another word he turned away.

He was impatient, suddenly, with this corpse of a town that had once been wild Abilene. Morning couldn't come too soon, and the train that would take him on to his destination, and whatever new chapter of his life he could expect to find there.

Carpetbag at his feet, braced against the jar of the platform between two swaying cars, Vern Balance watched the prairie wheeling past and wondered, half in earnest, if there could still be any longhorns left in the state of Texas. These swells of land seemed loaded down with them, each separate herd on its own holding ground, each attended by the tall-hatted figures of mounted men riding circle. And now and then—to be glimpsed briefly and then swept away again—the sprawl of a trail camp with its horse line, chuck wagon, scattering of trash, and the smoke of a cookfire spiraling toward the brassy, cloudless sky.

Like the camps of a besieging army, he thought; he'd have needed nothing more to tell him that Ellsworth—the center and focus of these encircling masses of grazing cattle—must lie just ahead.

For a man just out of prison, there was freedom and exhilaration in the pound of wheels punishing the rails—it eased, for a moment, the restless tensions that had made him desert his seat in the daycoach to come and stand out here. A stogie was clamped between his jaws but he had made no attempt to light it, enjoying instead the smells of sun-cooked grass and dust that rode the hot wind—even the occasional cloud of woodsmoke from the stack that engulfed him, or the stinging barrages of cinders swept up from the roadbed by suction of the rushing train.

To the south, dusty cottonwoods that marked the course of the Smoky Hill drew nearer, now, as they swung in parallel to the river's shallow course. They were getting close. A lonely blast of the whistle floated back; the engine's bell was signaling the station ahead as brakes began to grab. The door beside Balance was swung open and a brakeman went by, returning his nod curtly as he hustled forward.

Here, suddenly, was a tiny sprawl of buildings, set off by themselves; Balance had seen cribs before and he wondered idly if Ellsworth, like some other towns he'd known, relegated its red light district to a place just beyond the city limits. Moments later, with the train already slowing enough that he could have stepped down with scarcely any difficulty onto the right of way, the first scattered structures of the town proper slid by and gathered into the shape of a street—unpainted wooden hovels crowded absurdly cheek-by-jowl in the midst of the limitless Kansas prairie. And then, as the long boxlike depot drew alongside, throwing back echoes of jangling bell and escaping steam, he picked up his bag and swung off onto the platform before the wheels had ground completely to a halt.

He stood amid the smells of steam and heated metal and engine smoke, watching the bustle of station activity as he fired up his stogie and got his bearings. It appeared that Ellsworth had been laid out to straddle the Kansas Pacific's right of way, forming a plaza that was as wide as two ordinary streets, with the town's business houses lining either side of it and the depot and tracks and switch occupying the center. Anyone could guess that life here depended on the railroad.

Even so, the unloading of passengers and the discharge of freight from the single boxcar took little time. Within minutes the bell was clanging again; with a bang of couplings the train jerked into motion. As the last car slid by, the graceless line of structures along the north side of the plaza was revealed through a dissolving streamer of pungent woodsmoke.

Balance looked them over as he worked at his cigar, reading the identifying signs painted either on their false fronts or on boards that jutted out over the crooked sidewalk. Finally, not finding any that interested him, he carried his bag through the depot waiting room and out the other door. There, he could see a second row of buildings lying opposite.

Almost immediately he spotted the one he was looking for. A long minute, he frowned thoughtfully through the smoke of his cigar as he marked it for future reference; despite its false front it obviously was no more than a single story high, just as flimsily constructed and as devoid of paint as any of its neighbors. What had taken his eye was the name painted in letters a foot tall: GLENNON'S ORIENTAL PALACE. The beer shields on either side of the door identified it as a saloon. He could count three others in the same row and the same block.

Beyond their roofs he could see a hint of cottonwood heads lining the banks of the Smoky Hill south of town; but here on the plaza there was not a tree in the whole wide expanse of rutted earth—no shelter against the brutal Kansas sun. A few horses drooped their heads at the tie racks. As he watched, three riders wearing the steeple hats of the Texas trail herds jogged in from the west—from the holding grounds, or perhaps from the shipping pens which must lie in that direction. Dust, fogged up by their passage, drifted about them when the riders dismounted and tied and plodded into Beebe's Mercantile.

After that—stillness again, in the wake of the daily westbound: the quiet of a blistering summer morning settling over the immensity of the Kansas prairie. Vern Balance asked himself if it was possible to believe this torpid, heat-smothered village had actually taken over Abilene's role, of northern terminus for the long Texas trail . . .

One strangely familiar sight might have astonished him if Doc Radley hadn't prepared him for it: The Drovers Cottage, looming beyond a side street crossing south and west of where he stood, seemed none the worse for having been picked up and hauled sixty-odd miles and put down here in its new setting. A sprawling, three-storied frame building, it dominated just as it had in Abilene. In those former days, its lobby and veranda and bar had been almost the heart of the cattle trade, the place where drovers and buyers met and did their business. And though he had seen another, newer-looking hotel north of the tracks, behind him, it was to the Drovers Cottage that sentiment drew Vern Balance now—he had little enough in his pockets, but it should buy him a night's lodging.

He stepped down off the depot platform and turned in that direction. Despite the shading circle of his hatbrim, the glare of sunlight smashing down on him was blindingly, dazzlingly bright. A mean-looking dog came from somewhere to sniff at him suspiciously and then, when he ignored it, trotted away to flop in the shade beneath a water trough. Balance continued across the side street, and stepped up onto the gallery of the Drovers Cottage.

In barrel chairs ranged against the wall, four men with the look of stockmen and the sound of Texas in their voices had their heads together, apparently discussing the market. "By God!" he heard one declare loudly, slapping the side of a scuffed boot with a folded newspaper. "If I don't get a price I can least break even on, I figure I'm gonna have to hold them right here on the prairie and try for better in '74!"

"That's no sure answer!" another said darkly, shaking his head and using a sweat-blackened hat to fan himself. "A bad winter can hurt you, here on these plains. And who says next year's prices will be any better?"

"*Something's* got to give, because I've already done had all the slack took out of me!" And then the talk dropped off as the four of them watched Vern Balance walk past them. He didn't know them; he wondered with wry amusement if they thought he might be a buyer, with beef money in his pocket.

The twin glass doors were fastened wide, for circulation of air; after the blast of the sun, the lobby was pleasantly dark and cool, and vaguely luxuriant. His eyes adjusting, he saw the remembered lobby with its overstuffed chairs and dark woods and elegant brass fittings, and felt the carpet under his boots as he started for the desk. All around him, he could hear the sound of voices—sober, serious voices in the corners of the lobby and in the bar adjoining. No boisterous whiskey talk here, of trailhands cavorting in an end-of-trail saloon: These were the owners, the men with fortunes tied up in herds waiting on the prairie for buyers who so far had failed to appear. There would be little celebrating for these men: the burdens they bore were too soberingly heavy.

Vern Balance expected to see either Jim Gore or his wife at the desk, but the clerk on duty was a sallow-faced young man whom he didn't know. Yes, the clerk assured him, the hotel was well filled just now but there was a room available. He turned the desk register for the new guest and Balance set his bag down as he signed. He paid for a day in advance and took the tagged key that the clerk dropped on the desk in front of him. "Send up hot water," he ordered.

"Yes, sir. Right away, Mister Balance."

The number on the key tag led him to a front room on the second floor. All the rooms in the Drovers Cottage were of a good size and well fitted, in a manner to surprise anyone familiar with the usual drab prairie-town hotel. Balance set his bag on the commode, and tossed his hat on the bed as he looked around, then went to open the green shutters and let in light and air.

He had a good view, overlooking the plaza. Behind the business houses lining North Main he could see a scatter of private dwellings, but on the whole Ellsworth was a dreary place, trying to make a foothold for itself in a hard environment. Strange, he thought; a couple of years ago it would have spelled excitement—another boozy spree with other footloose young fellows like himself, another chance to try his skill and his luck across the green baize of a poker table.

It all seemed a long time ago.

He was still looking at the town when a tap at the door announced the maid with his hot water. Balance tossed the butt of his stogie through the window, and went to accept the steaming china pitcher. When he had washed away the soot and sweat of his train journey, he decided his cheeks could use a razor and got it from his bag, working up a lather with the bar soap he found on the commode.

Afterward, getting into a clean shirt, he paused to study for a moment the face that looked back at him from the mirror—the spare features, the sober gray eyes, the mouth that was not given much of late to smiling.

Howard Radley's remark yesterday, about the change in him, still troubled him a little. He supposed the change was there; actually, he couldn't recall very well what that young man of two years ago had been like: reckless for adventure, restless after a boring and uneventful Army hitch. Perhaps the truth was that something of himself had died in the same thunderclap of gunshot that killed Bud Spearman, over a card table in an Abilene saloon . . .

With these reflections darkening his thoughts, he hesitated a moment over his open carpetbag and from it lifted a contrivance of leather and wire—a shoulder harness, fitted out with a clip holster and a short-nosed Colt revolver. He drew out the gun, held it in his palm. Then, with a shake of the head, he replaced the weapon and returned gun and holster to the bag.

He had always been careful in his dress. He slipped into his coat, used a pair of military brushes on closecropped hair only now losing its prison look; drew on his hat. A final touch to his string tie and he was ready for the business that had brought him here.

On his way toward the stairs, he came upon a woman who was working with the key of her door. She had just got it open and as she straightened she looked around briefly; there was an impression of a slight figure, in a crisp white shirtwaist that looked somehow cool despite the heat of the hallway, and of large dark eyes under a soft mass of brown hair. Balance lifted a finger toward his hatbrim and, as he walked on, heard the door quietly close again. Only then, belatedly, a certain sense of familiarity about the face he had seen so briefly made him pause and turn. He frowned as he stood in the empty corridor, then shook his head. It must have been one of those tricks of imagination; she'd been attractive, and young, but he was quite sure he could never have seen her before.

Down through the lobby, then, to pause a moment in the street entrance while once again the heads of the loungers along the gallery lifted toward him in curiosity. A searing wind scoured the plaza, in a cloud of lifted dust and cinders. Someone swore halfheartedly and exclaimed, "D'you suppose it ever rains in this sonofabitching Kansas?"

Leaving the hotel, Vern Balance turned right, crossed the side street and stepped up onto the sidewalk fronting South Main's business places, grateful for the shade of the wooden awnings as he passed beneath them. There was a smell of dust, of horse urine beneath the tie racks, of stale sawdust and beer and tobacco smoke that gusted out through the open door of each saloon. Arriving at the eastern end of the block, and Glennon's Oriental Palace that he had earlier marked for attention, he stood aside as a couple of punchers came tromping out to a jingling of spur rowels, then pushed aside one of the green-painted, slotted half doors and entered.

It looked neither Oriental nor palatial. It was simply a long box of a room with a low, pressed-tin ceiling, its walls dingily papered. A bar with a row of soiled hand towels hanging from nails along the front of it occupied one long side. There was no backbar mirror. In a rear corner, beside a door to the back part of the building, a mechanical piano with cymbal and bass drum attachment stood silent and unused.

Balance saw a good scattering of customers at the bar and the tables, and yet the atmosphere was strangely subdued for such a place.

Though windows and street door stood wide open, heat that was a tangible thing hung trapped beneath the low ceiling. As soon as he had stepped inside, Vern Balance could feel the sweat begin to dribble down his ribs.

He turned to the bar, where a bartender with a black spit curl and a jaw like a shovel leaned boredly on his elbows, with little to do. A fly settled in a spot of spilled whiskey; the man slapped a palm against the wood and then lifted the thick fingers cautiously, checking his accuracy. He had missed. He wiped his hand on his apron as he turned a sullen stare on the newcomer.

"Is Glennon here?" Vern Balance asked.

The muddy eyes regarded him suspiciously. "Who wants him?"

"Glennon knows me."

Again the other took his time about an answer. "Never said when he'd be in," he muttered finally, and dismissed the question by turning to fill someone's glass. Balance watched him pour, set the bottle down and sweep the money into a cigar box placed under the counter for a till. Debating whether to let himself be angry at the man's rudeness, Balance shrugged and turned away. Plainly he could either wait or return later—it would make little sense to go hunting through an unfamiliar town. A small worm of frustration was starting to gnaw at him as he looked again, scowling, over the dingy barroom.

He found his eye drawn to a table where four men, with a bottle and glasses and a few coins and bills in front of them, seemed to be trying to breathe life into a desultory poker game. One, who sat with his back against the wall, was just gathering the deck and Balance watched with an experienced eye as the cards were skillfully shaped and then riffled together in a swift blurring.

The man was stocky, impeccably dressed; on the back of his dark head he wore the bowler that was almost the identifying badge of a professional gambler. Suddenly the hands paused in their work and Balance saw the other was staring directly at him down the length of the cluttered room, recognition striking both in the same moment. There seemed no point in avoiding a meeting, and Vern Balance headed that way, the players looking up as he came to a halt beside their table. He nodded to the one who held the cards.

"Ben," he said, "how are you?"

CHAPTER III

Ben Thompson—gambler, gunman, killer, ex-convict, ex-soldier for Maximilian—nodded curtly. Only the pale eyes, above the flowing black mustache and goatee and stubborn jaw, would tend to confirm a reputation of one of the most thoroughly dangerous men ever to come out of the state of Texas. Knowing his unpredictable temper, Vern Balance respected the man but knew enough to treat him warily.

"I'll be a sonofabitch!" Thompson said now. "When did they let you out?"

"Last week."

The chill eyes narrowed in calculation. "Let's see—how long were you up for?" Balance told him. "That long?" Ben Thompson grunted and shook his head. "I wouldn't have believed it. Well—time flies."

"Not where I've been!" Vern Balance said; and Ben Thompson, who had himself done time for a killing, in Huntsville Prison in Texas, appeared to agree. A gesture indicated the others about the table. "I guess you know the boys."

"I think so," Balance said, dredging up the names from memory as he nodded to Neil Kane and Cad Pierce—cronies of Thompson's, Texans also but, unlike him, dressed in the rough clothing of the cattle trail, with tall hats pushed back from sun-darkened faces. At the fourth man, though, he hesitated, not placing him until Thompson supplied a name: "This here's John Sterling."

They had never met but Balance knew of this John Sterling as a gambler with a reputation for winning on poor hands. He seemed to be winning here, for whatever that was worth; he was shaping up a slim stack of coins and greenbacks, and the eyes in the sallow face gave Balance the briefest of glances. "You're the one killed the Spearman kid."

It was a blunt statement of fact and Balance did not deny it.

Thompson had finished shuffling and was merely toying with the cards, pulling out the heart of the deck in his tapered fingers and softly slapping it together again, over and over, while his eyes studied Balance. "How long you been in Ellsworth?"

"I just got in today."

Neil Kane said, "Then you've missed Clayt Spearman by about twenty-four hours. Him and that trail boss—Telford, I think his name is. I understand they taken off for Wichita or someplace, thought they had a line there on a buyer for their cattle. They could be back any time."

They were all watching Balance, as though curious for his reaction. He kept his face and voice expressionless as he said, "That's their business." Kane started to say something else but saw his look and let it go, pouring himself a drink instead. Turning again to Thompson, Vern Balance asked, "Is Billy here with you?"

"He's around somewhere. Came up with Neil's outfit." The set of his mouth, and his carefully casual manner, gave warning that his brother was something Ben Thompson preferred not to discuss just then. It suited Balance, since he had asked about Billy Thompson merely out of politeness. Now he pulled out the empty chair Ben pointed to, but hesitated. "I wasn't looking for a game."

"Don't worry—you haven't found one." Thompson's voice held boredom and disgust and a barely leashed anger. He flung down the deck, carelessly, so that the cards spread across the baize in a smear of patterned backs; picking up his money, he shoved it into a pocket without bothering to count it.

Vern Balance eased into the chair, seeing the game was obviously breaking up. "Not much going on? From the train, it looked like quite a few outfits around."

"Over 150,000 head of longhorns right now, they tell me, out on the range," Thompson answered sourly. "But with no buyers, there's hardly a dollar in cash money going the rounds. The owners are on tick to the storekeepers, and the crews hang around kicking their heels while they wait to get paid. Doesn't make much in the way of pickings for a card dealer."

Neil Kane hefted the bottle. "I brung a herd up from Austin—and here I sit playing for pennies while I wait for somebody to take it off my hands. Even at these prices you can't give the damned stuff away!" He drank directly from the bottle, wiped its neck on his thumb and offered Balance the whiskey, but the latter shook his head.

Thompson looked at him sharply as he reached past, took the bottle himself, and refilled his own glass—if the sight of Vern Balance turning down both whiskey and cards caused him to wonder, he made no comment. Throwing off the drink, Ben Thompson said gruffly, "There has to be a break, sooner or later! I come to Ellsworth thinking I might open a place, but if things don't happen pretty quick I may move on. Try my luck in Colorado—Leadville, maybe."

Cad Pierce said, "According to the newspaper, back in Chicago they're saying this cattle market is just the first sign. The whole country's headed for what they call a recession, before '73 is over."

There was a silence. Vern Balance realized these men shared the same poor mood that he'd detected earlier at the Drovers Cottage. The very air of the room was freighted with sour discontent, heavy as the heat that frayed at a man's nerves.

Shifting in his chair, he looked around. "Joe Glennon doesn't seem to be doing too badly."

"As well as anyone, I guess," Ben Thompson said. He indicated the bottle. "Stocks better liquor than some of the other places. I don't know how much of a businessman he is." He added: "Seems like you and him were pretty thick back in Abilene. Weren't you supposed to be going into partnership, once?"

"It never got that far," Balance said briefly. He was watching the bartender wiping a mop rag over the polished wood. Without a break in his movements, the man deftly scooped up the coins a pair of trailhands had just dropped, in payment for their drinks; but though his fist passed above the open cigar-box till, Balance didn't see the thick fingers open. Instead the hand dipped quickly toward his trousers pocket, to reappear empty. As it did the bartender's head turned furtively, a glance shooting from under the spit curl plastered to his sweating forehead, as though checking that no one had observed. Aside from Vern Balance, apparently no one had.

Mildly interested in this petty thievery, Balance set himself to keep an eye on the man, as the disgruntled talk continued and the bottle went the rounds of the table. Twice within a short quarter hour he saw money from the bar make the trip to the pocket under the apron, bypassing its proper destination in the till. Once he started to call the others' attention but on some obscure impulse held his tongue.

Irritable, and always made restless by waiting, he decided at last he had had enough and pushed his chair back, ready to make some excuse and leave. As he did, angry voices began to shout thinly in the street outside.

A man came bursting through the batwings and, after a brief glance about, came heading directly toward the table where Thompson sat. "Ben, there's trouble!" he said excitedly. "It's Happy Jack Morco— he's trying to lay the arm on Billy!"

At the news, the Texan's face suffused with quick color; a single harsh obscenity, and the chair was clattering to the floor behind him as he lunged to his feet. Kane and Pierce were only a trifle slower; they followed close behind as Thompson started for the door, his informant trailing. In a general scraping of chairs and shuffling of boots, the likelihood of excitement drew the saloon crowd to get a look at what was going on.

John Sterling had kept his place, however; he had the abandoned deck and was casually dealing himself poker hands, and Balance's question drew an indifferent glance from him. "Who's Happy Jack Morco?"

The gambler shrugged. "Deputy city marshal," he said briefly. "Ain't the first trouble them Thompsons have got into with the Ellsworth police." His attention returned to the cards he was dealing, and Vern Balance left him. A clot of men had gathered in the doorway and on the sidewalk outside. Curious, he pushed through to the edge of the wooden arcade and saw at once what was happening, in the dust and fierce sunlight only a few yards from where he stood.

Anyone would have known these Thompsons were related, even though Billy had a few rangy inches on his elder brother and his hair and eyes and mustache were lighter. He had the Thompson temper— on a shorter fuse if anything, and under weaker self-control. Vern Balance, who had always held a wary respect for Ben, never felt he wanted any more to do with Billy than he had to; he had seldom seen the man when he wasn't drinking, and whiskey could turn him slobbering, deadly mean.

He had at least one murder warrant out on him in Texas, which made it impossible for him to go back there; so he spent his time hanging out in the lawless Indian Nations or—when he could—trailing around after his more famous brother. Near Balance's own age—twenty-six, perhaps—Billy stood now on uncertain legs, hatless and with hair streaming into his sweaty face. A belt and holstered gun, that he was always ready to use, were strapped high about his middle; Ben gripped him by one arm, as if to steady him, and it was Ben's voice that sounded thinly against the stillness: "The hell with this, Morco. He's not hurting anybody."

"That's for me to judge!" The speaker had a hogleg pistol naked in his hand and a metal star pinned askew to the front of his unbuttoned vest. To Vern Balance this Happy Jack Morco had all the look of an ignorant small-town bully. Swarthy, mean-eyed under a thatch of drab brown hair that stood up like a rooster's comb, he had a mouth that knew only how to sneer. "The man's defyin' the law. You know damn' well there's a town ord'nance to keep you Texas riffraff from wearin' your artillery on the streets!"

"So today he forgot to turn in his gun," Ben Thompson said patiently. "He's been drinking a little and it slipped his mind. But, what the hell? He's not going to use it."

"Damn right he ain't—because I'm takin' it!" An audience, and a gun in his own fist, apparently fed the man's arrogance. "What's more, I'm takin' him to court on a charge of drunk *and* disorderly. You watch out, boy, I don't haul you in too, for interfering with a police officer!"

Vern Balance listened in cold amazement. You didn't talk like that to Ben Thompson! The latter was plainly holding himself in by an effort of will, but the angry color darkening his cheeks should have been enough to make a smarter man than this Happy Jack Morco think twice. Balance could only wonder at the town authorities who would choose such a clod to enforce its law.

There was a tremor of contained fury in Ben Thompson's voice as he said, "You'd do just about anything for a two-dollar fee, wouldn't you?"

The deputy's sneer grew broader. "You reb bastards gonna learn this is Kansas, and you ain't cocks of the walk around here." He turned to Billy, the heavy revolver waggled in his fist. "Come on, boy!" he ordered loudly. "Just hand over that gun."

Billy Thompson swore, and lunging unexpectedly out of Ben's grasp swung a drunken fist at Morco's jaw.

It was a feeble blow, poorly aimed, that missed its target and barely grazed the man's chest. But the force of his blow flung Billy half around, and for a moment Ben Thompson had a problem keeping his brother on his feet. Morco had fallen back a step; Balance, glancing at him, saw the hot shine of fury in his eyes. And then he saw the gun drop level against Billy Thompson's back and realized, with a clutch of horror, that in another instant Morco was going to work the trigger.

It was useless to shout a warning. Scarcely thinking he moved forward, closing the distance in a couple of strides that brought him up on Morco's blind side; his quick grab trapped the officer's wrist and twisted it so that when the gun exploded it was pointing harmlessly at the white-hot sky. Startling echoes bounced off the building fronts and then were silenced.

Ben Thompson was staring, though Billy seemed oblivious to the thing that had nearly happened to him; the crowd on the sidewalk, watching, appeared stunned. Morco was first to recover. He loosed a scream of rage and would have pulled away if Balance hadn't kept a grip on his gun wrist. "Easy!" He tried with words to penetrate the lawman's skull. "I don't think you really want to shoot a man in the back."

That appeared to calm Morco a little; he looked at Billy Thompson as though seeming to realize, for the first time, what he had almost done. Scowling, he pulled loose and Balance let him go, though he felt his stomach muscles tighten as he saw the gun swing to point vaguely at his own middle. "And just who the hell are you? I ain't seen you around."

Before there was time to answer, a newcomer shouldered out through the crowd and Balance moved quickly to get a view of him— a slight, neatly dressed man, with thinning hair and full mustache and beard touched with gray; there was the look of a businessman about him, though he held himself with almost a military alertness. Sunlight flashed on the sheriff's badge pinned to his coat, but Balance could see no gun. Mild, intelligent blue eyes took in the situation. Turning to Happy Jack Morco, the sheriff said, "I heard a gun."

"No concern of yours, Whitney," the deputy marshal told him bluntly. "It's a town matter."

He considered this a moment; he let his glance touch Vern Balance briefly and then looked at the Thompsons. Ben was a little white, but Billy seemed befuddled still. Whitney asked, "Anyone hurt, Ben?"

"I told you to keep out of this!" Morco snarled. He turned again on the stranger. "You! I'm still waiting to hear your name!" Vern Balance, with a shrug, gave it but couldn't see any reaction. "You got a gun under that coat?"

Balance made no move to show him. "If I had," he retorted, not quite able to keep the contempt he felt out of his voice, "you could have been dead by now . . ."

Ben Thompson addressed the sheriff. "Cap, Billy took a swing at him and the sonofabitch was going to drill him where he stood. Drunk as Billy is, if Morco hadn't been stopped it would have been murder."

"That is a damned lie!" Morco bawled hotly, and drew a chorus of boos from the onlookers that turned his face to scarlet. He let an angry glare rake the crowd. "I'm authorized to keep the peace, south of the K.P. tracks here in Ellsworth. I'll shoot who I have to—and I ain't answerable to any of you. Including *you,* Whitney!" He stepped and laid a hand on Billy Thompson's shoulder. "This man's under arrest, for wearing a gun in defiance of a town ord'nance and resisting an officer. I'm taking him to the judge."

Sheriff Whitney pursed his lips as he gave Ben Thompson a worried look. "I guess that's the way it is, Ben. Like me to come along?"

Thompson's eyes were terrible, but he shook his head. He turned to Morco. "Let's get it over with," he gritted.

"First, I'll take the gun." Happy Jack Morco held out his hand and with a grim expression Ben Thompson slipped the weapon from his brother's holster and passed it over.

Morco was almost beside himself, in his triumph over the Thompsons. He showed all his teeth in a grin as he snatched the revolver and shoved it behind his belt. And he included Vern Balance in his

arrogance. "I'm gonna remember *you*, mister!" he promised haught-
ily. "You just better think I will!" Not waiting for an answer he swung
away to where the Thompsons stood waiting.

For the moment Billy was subdued and docile enough. Morco
gave the prisoner's shoulder an open-palmed shove that nearly
knocked him sprawling. "Get moving!" he ordered. He was swag-
gering and brandishing the hogleg revolver as he herded the Thompsons over the open stretch of dust toward North Main, across the
sun-shimmering rails.

CHAPTER IV

The sheriff shook his head and muttered darkly, "Damn, I wish I knew what to do about that! We have a hard enough time keeping good relationships between the town, and the men who bring business here!" He turned a considering look, then, on the stranger. "Your name's Balance? I'm Chauncey Whitney."

Balance said, "Seems to me I've heard of you. As I recall, you've been sheriff here ever since Ellsworth County was organized. And weren't you with Forsyth, that time at the Arickaree?"

The other inclined his head. "An old soldier, that's me—it's why my friends call me 'Cap.' But since the war I'm just a storekeeper, except that we've had trouble keeping the sheriff's office filled and I try to do what I can. Sometimes, like just now, it ain't enough." He added: "I guess you're a friend of Ben and Billy Thompson . . ."

"I've known them awhile," Balance said carefully, as they turned together to move out of the street where they were at the shriveling mercy of the sun.

"I like Ben," the sheriff said. "He has a savage temper, but he's honest and makes no bones about what he is; and I think he's really trying, this summer, not to cause any trouble. Billy, of course, is something else again. But so far Ben's been keeping him in line pretty well."

"How long will that last—with somebody like Happy Jack Morco around for him to tangle with? Where did the town have to look to find itself that kind of a lawman?"

"I'll tell you where they got him!" Neil Kane leaned against one of the props of the arcade fronting Joe Glennon's saloon—a dark-haired six-footer, in a savage mood as he volunteered to answer Balance's question. "Morco showed up from nowhere earlier in the summer, claiming to be from California and bragging about the dozen men he's wanted for killing out there. Right after he hit town he got picked up for vagrancy—and a week later he'd been put on the police force!"

Vern Balance looked to the sheriff, who merely shrugged in confirmation. "It's got to be a problem," Whitney pointed out, "finding the men to keep the lid on a town that's swarming with angry Texans, most of them with nothing to do and no money in their pockets. At the moment, Ellsworth has just four men on its police force, including the chief marshal—a man named John Norton . . ."

"Norton?" Balance repeated. "I think I must have known him at Abilene. A special deputy to Hickok, hired to patrol the brothels— they called him Brocky Jack. Is that the one?"

"The same," Neil Kane told him. "Brocky Jack Norton and Happy Jack Morco—there's a real pair for you. And the other two—Hogue and DeLong—they're no better. You take scum like Morco, hang a badge and a gun on him and give him the license to swagger around town making better men lick his boots—he's still nothing but scum! How long do they expect us to put up with it?"

Whitney gave the Texan a hard look but only shook his head again, and drawing a handkerchief from his pocket mopped the beaded sweat from his forehead. "I don't know," the sheriff admitted. "If there was just a break in the heat—or the market for these long-horns could only pick up! That's what has every man's temper on edge."

The sheriff put away the handkerchief, looked at a heavy silver watch. "Well, the wife's already waiting dinner." As he pocketed the watch he appraised Balance with those mild, intelligent blue eyes. "Occurs to me where I heard your name before. None of my business, of course, but that trial in Abilene did cause considerable stir. I don't suppose I'm the first to remind you—"

"That I'm apt to be seeing Clayt Spearman, if I stay in your town long?" Balance finished for him. "No, you're only about the fourth. Thanks anyway?"

For another moment the eyes held him. Then Chauncey Whitney said shortly, "Just so you're aware." He nodded, and abruptly turned and left them.

"A good man," Neil Kane said. "Trouble is, being county sheriff he's got no authority here in town." He pushed away from the post where he had been leaning, his brooding stare swinging once more across the plaza where the Thompsons and the deputy marshal had vanished.

Noontime had shadows stretching more briefly, now, across the dust; a wind that appeared to blow from the heart of the swollen sun itself passed briefly, and swept a stinging yellow curtain ahead of it. The Texan said, "I better ease on over, see how it's going with Ben and Billy in that courtroom. You, though—it's just as well that you stay away from Morco."

Balance answered shortly, "I haven't the least interest in Happy Jack Morco."

"He has in *you*, I think."

"Then if we happen to show in the same place, at the same time, I suppose he'll make of it what he wants."

"Well, so far," Kane told him, "nobody's cared to take him on— Ben could likely handle him but he doesn't want to make a fight of it; and the rest of us are leery in case the twelve dead men in California should turn out to be something more than brag. But the way he's going, one of these days somebody may have to call his hand. If it should turn out to be you—good luck!"

Glennon still had not returned; the larcenous bartender dismissed Balance's question with a curt shake of the head. Cad Pierce was standing at the bar and he signaled to Balance but the latter once more declined the offer of a drink. Disgruntled over the waste of so much time, he returned to his room at the Drovers Cottage to prepare for dinner.

The shirt he had put on clean was already sweated through and he stripped out of it, crumpled and flung it on the bed, and got another from his carpetbag. But this time, remembering Happy Jack Morco's half-veiled threats, he also took out the clip holster and revolver and strapped them in place, afterward checking the hang of his coat to make sure no betraying bulge might hint he deliberately violated the town's law against carrying weapons.

He still wanted no trouble with anyone in Ellsworth, during the time he expected to be here; but as he had told Doc Radley, he meant to protect himself.

When he left his room, the young woman he had seen earlier was just passing through the long corridor toward the stairs; he locked his own door, pocketed the key, and followed at a distance of several paces. Because of the pile of the carpet underfoot, Balance was certain she had no awareness anyone was behind her. He allowed himself to enjoy the pleasing picture of her—the confident set of her head and carriage of her shoulders, the soft-looking brown curls that bobbed at her neck with each quick step, the contour of waist and flaring hipline and the unconscious grace of carriage. He was still a little distance behind and above her as she started down the steps, and when she turned at the landing he got a brief look at her face and once again was struck by a disturbing sense of familiarity. And yet, he was convinced that if he had ever seen this girl before today, he would certainly have remembered her.

The hotel seemed to have come alive now, with approach of the dinner hour. He heard voices rising from the lobby, and there was the bustle and chime of dishes and silverware beyond the archway leading into the dining room. Behind the desk Balance saw the familiar face of Lou Gore, the wife of the proprietor, as she conferred with the desk clerk on some matter; he nodded and got a brief frown, as though she found difficulty in placing him.

In the dining-room entrance, he found the girl had halted uncertainly and as he came up behind her he saw that the room appeared almost completely full, busy with talk and the sounds of eating and with waitresses moving among the tables. As the girl hesitated, looking for one that was not occupied, a couple of men in the garb of drovers pushed by into the room; they were arguing loudly and seemed not to notice her, but she drew hastily out of their way and in so doing backed into Vern Balance.

He caught her arm to steady her; she gasped and pulled away, turning hastily. Her face was pink with embarrassment as she exclaimed faintly, "I'm sorry!"

Vern Balance had quickly dropped his hand again. He smiled reassuringly. "Looks like this place is pretty busy." He added, "I think I see a free table for you. May I?" And when she nodded, still flustered, he took her elbow and guided her to it, and drew out a chair for her to sit.

"That was real kind of you," she said.

"Not at all." Touching his hatbrim to her, he turned to hunt out a table for himself.

At his elbow he heard her say, "I don't believe there's a single one left. Would you like to share mine?"

Balance looked at her. He said carefully, "Just so you understand I didn't plan this."

"Of course not," she said, and smiled. The smile was friendly and yet without any trace of boldness; it simply lit up her face and warmed the level regard of her brown eyes. "You'd better sit down or you'll get nothing to eat at all." She indicated the chair across from her; he could see there was no ring on her finger.

The Drovers Cottage used real linen in its dining room, good cutlery, and china and water glasses that glinted in the light. As Vern Balance seated himself and straightened from leaning to place his hat on the floor beneath his chair, he glanced past the girl's head to the lobby entrance; Lou Gore stood in the arch with arms folded beneath her matronly bosom, watching their table with an expression of cold suspicion.

Balance told the girl, "If looks could kill, I wouldn't give much for my chances just now. Mrs. Gore is letting me know she doesn't think much of this."

"Lou Gore is an old dear," she answered. "But I'm sure she doesn't approve of me dining with a man I haven't been introduced to."

"Then I'd better fix that. I'm Vern Balance."

She bobbed her head in mock courtesy. "How do you do? And I'm Tess Spearman." It was only the arrival of the waitress, just then, that kept her from noticing the horror in his stare.

He covered up somehow. After all, the name itself wasn't conclusive, although that troubling sense of familiarity in the first look he'd had at her returned now to bother him still more. He had to know for certain, and when the waitress had taken their orders and left again he pursued the matter further: "You're never from this part of the world—not with that accent. That's Texas, if I ever heard it."

"I don't suppose there'd be any use my ever trying to pretend," she said. "I'm a ranch girl, Mister Balance—from Uvalde County. My papa is Clayton Spearman. We own the Rafter 7, down that way." Balance nodded. "Heard of it."

So there was no longer any question. She was Clayt Spearman's daughter, and the sister of the man he had killed two years ago in Abilene; the resemblance to both was so strong that he wondered, now, how he could have missed it—those Spearmans were a handsome family! But then, how was it that she showed no sign of recognizing the name of her brother's killer?

He calculated swiftly. Tess Spearman seemed to him barely over twenty, if she was that; two years ago, she'd have been little more than a child, and in faraway Texas it might very well be that she had been protected from learning very much of the details about what had happened to her handsome brother—including the name of the man who shot him. The breath was shallow in his throat as he thought, now, what the reaction could have been when he identified himself a moment ago.

He wanted to know more, and asked, "Are you in Ellsworth by yourself? This seems a long way from home."

"The farthest I've ever been," she agreed, turning the stem of her water glass between her fingers. "Papa and I came by steamboat to St. Louis, and then here on the cars to meet our trail herd. We mean to go on to Denver and the Coast for a visit as soon as the cattle are sold, but this is taking longer than he had expected."

Balance nodded. "I'd heard the market was a little slow."

"It's terrible—the worst it's been since we started shipping from Kansas. Papa and Ernie Telford, our trail boss, are traveling around right now, trying to see if they can't scare up a buyer. And meanwhile I'm stuck at the Drovers Cottage—sort of under Mrs. Gore's wing until they get back. That's why she watches me so close. She feels responsible for me."

Balance looked again toward the lobby doorway. "Well, she's gone about her business; so maybe she doesn't think you're in too great danger with me, after all."

"Maybe *you're* a cattle buyer, Mister Balance?" the girl suggested, looking at him hopefully. "If you're in the market, there's twenty-five hundred head of prime longhorn beef wearing the Rafter 7 brand, grazing four miles north and west of town."

He shook his head. "I'm afraid that's not my line," he said, and did not have to say any more because the waitress returned just then with their orders.

They made only small talk as they ate, and not much of that, with the noise of the room about them and noontime glare outside the windows. When he had finished Balance insisted on paying for both meals. Rising, hat in hand, he said, "If I can get my business in Ellsworth finished tonight, I'll probably be leaving on the morning train; so, chances are you won't be seeing me again. I'd just like to say I never had a nicer dinner companion."

She smiled up at him. "Thank you," she said, and offered him her hand. He took it briefly, and then walked away from her and through the doorway into the lobby.

He was still thinking of her and failed to respond to the sound of his own name; turning, he saw Lou Gore bearing down on him. She could be the soul of kindness itself—in particular, to a Texas cow-puncher who found himself far from home and ill or down on his luck; but just now there was stern seriousness in her manner. "I think I'll have to ask you, just what was going on in there?"

"Nothing at all," Balance assured her. "You can blame the fact that your dining room is doing too good a business—that's why we had to share a table."

Not satisfied, the woman studied his face closely. "Does that girl know who you are?" she demanded.

"I didn't see any reason to tell her."

She shook her head, frowning darkly. "You understand, her pa's more or less left her in my charge. She's a real sweet youngster; if I thought there was any chance of her being hurt—"

"Not by me," Vern Balance answered soberly. "God knows I've hurt that family enough! Anyway, I don't expect I'll be running into her again; so, you can ease your mind on that score."

The woman's eyes held his own. "I hope so!" she said bluntly. But she didn't press him further.

CHAPTER V

Balance had to make two more tries before, just at sundown, he found the man he was looking for.

With day's end the edge of the heat had become blunted, but still a tide of warm dry air flowed sluggishly across the Kansas prairie and through the town. Lights already bloomed in windows, and cookfires marked the trail camps that ringed the village like a besieging army. As he once more approached the Oriental Palace, a last spray of lemon-yellow afterglow hung in the western sky and the saloons along South Main were tuning up.

The level of sound seemed to have mounted by several decibels; the racket that poured out of open saloon doorways met the arriving sound of hoofs stirring the dust as new recruits, in ever greater numbers, poured in from the holding grounds. Glennon's business, too, had picked up. Two bartenders were busy, and the long, low-ceilinged room housed a hubbub of loud voices, pitched now above the noise of the mechanical piano that was racketing away with drum and cymbal attachment beating out an insistent rhythm. When Balance entered he saw his man at once.

Joe Glennon was massive, corpulent, possessed of a booming voice and laugh and a boisterous good humor which he could use to overwhelm another person. He was talking to someone now and Vern Balance, coming up behind him, could almost feel the weight of the fleshy hand, with the moist butt of a fat cigar between two of its fingers, that he laid on the other's shoulder—Glennon could not seem to converse without using his hands, kneading and pummeling and prodding with palms that were usually moist with sweat. The same bartender was on duty, and now as he sighted Balance he leaned forward and said something to his employer. Glennon quickly turned.

He was prepared with his habitual smile, that bunched the thick flesh of his cheeks and lent his black eyes a look of good fellowship; but when he saw Vern Balance the smile slipped a little and the eyes changed and became carefully watchful. For a moment Balance thought the man had decided not to recognize him; but then, dismissing the one he'd just been talking to, Glennon came toward him saying, "Well!"—a word that could mean anything. "When Nat told me someone had been in," he continued, "it never occurred to me it might be you."

"No?"

Balance found his hand engulfed in a sweaty paw; he felt his shoulder being massaged and moved slightly to free it. "I guess I took it for granted you still had time left to serve. How the hell long *were* you in?"

"Two years, to the day," Balance said. "Every day of it."

"And now you're out. That calls for a drink."

"If you don't mind, I'd rather talk business."

"Oh?" The black eyes studied him shrewdly, though the smile remained. "Yes, I guess I see what you mean. Well, then let's go in my office . . ."

The hand was at his shoulder again, turning and pointing him toward the door at the rear of the smoke-blue room. They walked back there, threading a way through the crowd with Glennon, a step behind, throwing out his jovial greeting to various acquaintances— he was a popular man with his customers, obviously. They passed the deafening thump and crash of the mechanical piano; Glennon reached around Balance and opened the door, and when he closed it behind them the uproar slightly abated.

Beyond the partition was a storage space, dimly lighted by a bracket lamp that revealed the stacks of empty beer barrels and liquor cases and the piles of accumulated trash—broken tables and chairs and other such wreckage. One corner had been enclosed to serve as an office; when they entered this and Glennon turned up the lamp, Balance saw a cluttered roll-top desk with a swivel chair, an overstuffed leather armchair, a brass spittoon, a dusty file cabinet. An open window let in a faint breath of air, laden with the smell of dust and a hint of stockyard odors, to stir the odors of Glennon's gross and sweaty body. The monotonous thump of the mechanical piano came to them, only a little muffled by the partition wall.

Glennon waved his guest to the armchair and took his own place at the desk. He flipped up the lid of a box of cigars, saying, "Try one of these. They're my favorite brand."

Balance eyed the cigars and though they tempted him he shook his head. He was down to the last of his supply of stogies, but he had no impulse to develop tastes that were beyond what he could afford.

He said, "You seem to handle a pretty good business here. How long you been open?"

"Since May." Glennon hawked and spat into the cuspidor, returned the cigar butt to a corner of his mouth, swiveled the chair about, and placed both hands upon his thighs as he looked at his guest. "I suppose I get my share of the trade," he said. "But expenses are high, and things ain't quite like you knew them at Abilene. The cattle market—"

The market—it was all anyone could talk about. Balance held his tongue. Glennon shook his head, mouthing the stub of cigar. "At least, I'm glad right now I haven't got my money tied up in Texas longhorn cattle!"

"*Your* money?" Balance said quietly.

"Of course, of course—part of it's yours. You didn't suppose I'd forgotten?"

"You might have thought *I* had. I was pretty drunk when I handed it over—but not *that* drunk. It isn't every poker game where a man gets up from the table a three thousand dollar winner . . . and he's not apt to forget what he did with it, either."

Suddenly Joe Glennon was frowning; it was as though the easy public smile had slipped from him like a mask, nakedly revealing a second face beneath. The black eyes had taken on a hard luster.

"In another minute," the fat man said, "you're going to be accusing me of bad faith. At the time I had every intention of honoring our agreement, about going partners in a place of our own there in Abilene. I had to take a trip to Kansas City and then on to Chicago, hoping to arrange the rest of the financing; but I didn't have any luck there. And when I got back I heard you'd got yourself convicted in a killing over a poker game, and sent to state's prison. What was I supposed to do?"

"Let's forget the money, for a moment," Balance said. "Now that you've brought it up, I'd like to talk a little about that game where I killed Bud Spearman."

"I don't know anything about it," the other said quickly. "I was in Chicago . . ."

"Yes, you keep pointing that out. But a friend of yours was there. A gambler by the name of Rand Harker . . ."

He was watching the man's eyes; he saw them grow careful. "Harker? Name sounds familiar," Glennon said finally.

"I'm glad it does. Because, it occurred to me afterward that I'd once seen the pair of you together. In a bar having a drink, as I remember."

"Could be," Glennon said shortly, his voice hard edged. "I've agreed I knew the man. I got to know quite a few people that summer in Abilene, while I was trying to raise the backing to start up a business. Look, Balance! What are you trying to say?"

"Why, I was telling you about killing Bud Spearman. After all, I've put in a couple of years behind bars, thinking about very little else. I started to say, there were six of us at that table in the Alamo, including Spearman and me and his father's trail boss—a man named Telford. And Rand Harker, of course . . ."

Glennon had taken the cigar stub from his lips. The gross features looked now as though they had been carved out of some solid material. "So?"

"So just this: If it wasn't for the whiskey I was drinking, I should have known that my luck was running too good that night. It wasn't until after it was too late—after the shooting—that I was able to piece things together and remember that the one who was dealing, and slipped the extra spade king into my hand that started the shooting, was your friend Harker."

"Now, wait a minute!" the fat man cut in. "Are you trying to connect *me* with it, somehow?"

"Harker didn't know me, or Bud Spearman either so far as I'm aware of. There was absolutely no reason for him to have fed me winning cards, and then topped them with the one that would blow the hand wide open. At the very least it would have been enough to discredit me and force me to leave town as a blackleg; as things actually worked out, young Spearman was pushed past the boiling point and went for his gun, and it's only by an accident that I wasn't the one who ended up lying in the sawdust, with a bullet in me."

"And you've decided," Glennon said roughly, "that I put Harker up to it—as a way to get out of repaying your three thousand."

"Men have been killed for a lot less."

The other's big head wagged slowly from side to side. He dropped the soggy end of his cigar into the spittoon by the desk. "I don't find this very amusing," he said; and, at something in the quality of his voice, Vern Balance took the precaution of reaching inside his coat and bringing out the snubnosed revolver.

He caught the flicker of shocked surprise in the fat man's stare, but that was the only reaction. Balance laid the gun on the wide leather arm of the chair, close to his fingers. "I'm not laughing very loud myself," he said grimly. "For two years I've had to live with the fact that I snuffed out a life. Knowing it was a drunken accident doesn't seem to help any—not even thinking that Bud Spearman may have been set up as part of a scheme to get me killed."

Perhaps it was the breathless heat of the room, but he could see a film of sweat suddenly shining at the other's hairline. Glennon was looking at the gun; now he lifted his stare again. "Has it occurred to you," he said, "you might have the whole thing backwards? If there was a plot, how do you know it wasn't aimed at Spearman? After all, *he's* the one that ended up dead. And he was a worthless brat, spoiled rotten and hated by his own crew. How do you know that trail boss of his father's didn't set the game up as a way to get rid of him? Because, that's exactly how it turned out."

"Naturally, in two years I've thought of that," Balance told him patiently. "Drunk as I was that night, I still remember that Telford kept goading the kid over his losses until he was worked up to the edge of his temper. And yet, when those two kings turned up and Spearman called me a cheat and went for his gun, Telford did everything he could to hold him back and prevent a shooting. What's more, I wasn't even armed—and Telford couldn't have helped knowing it. Once Spearman started shooting, I had to grab a gun out of the holster of the man sitting next to me. I was so confused and befuddled I still don't really remember firing the shot that killed him; but I have to believe what all the witnesses said."

Joe Glennon touched his tongue to his lips. He tried another tack. "Instead of coming after me, why didn't you get ahold of Harker? Looks like *he's* the one you should be talking to . . ."

"I never saw the man again. He disappeared and couldn't be called as a witness at my trial. But a year later—in prison—I heard on the grapevine that his body had been found lodged in the willows along the Smoky Hill. There was a bullet in him. I can't help wondering if he didn't return for his payoff, or try for blackmail—and that's what he got instead!"

The two of them stared at each other above the gun lying on the chair arm, through a silence that was broken only by the fat man's asthmatic breathing and, from the barroom, the monotonous pulsing of the mechanical piano's bass drum attachment. "So what it comes down to," Glennon said finally, "you've got no proof of any kind. In your own head, you've built a fair case against me, but I deny it in every particular. Now what do you do—shoot me? It won't bring the kid back to life; and it certainly won't cut any ice with Clayt Spearman, if he should ever manage to get his hands on you.

"I knew nothing at all about that poker game. I was five hundred miles away at the time. As for Rand Harker, I had talked to him just the once, for perhaps half an hour: I was looking for a partner and a backer—but it took me no longer than that, to know he wasn't the one I needed . . ."

Listening, Vern Balance all at once was faced with the fact that Glennon either was telling the truth, or was the smoothest liar he had ever encountered. He had been morally certain that, faced with the charge, the man would betray himself; now he was experiencing the first strong doubt, and it left him baffled and frustrated.

And what difference, after all, could it have made to prove his suspicions? He had been wrong to think it would erase his own guilt. His whole way of existence had been to blame. Had he not been in a saloon, gambling and drinking and wasting his life, Bud Spearman would not have forfeited his.

Glennon must have seen the run of thought reflected in his face, for the fat man's tensions seemed to relax. Waiting, he selected a fresh cigar from the box at his elbow, bit off the end, and spat it into the cuspidor as he dug into a waistcoat pocket for a match. Not finding any, he turned and slid open a drawer in the front of the desk.

Jarred out of his thoughts, Vern Balance said sharply, "Hold it!"

The gun was in his hand again, and leveled. As Glennon froze, Balance leaned forward, shoving his arm away, and reached into the drawer himself. Mouth gone hard, he brought out an ugly little two-shot derringer.

Glennon did not turn a hair. Under Balance's angry glare he merely shrugged as he pointed out, "A man with a gun pointed at his face has to do *something* . . ." For a moment they tested each other. Then, with an angry grimace, Balance holstered his own gun while he gave attention to unloading the captured weapon; he pocketed the shells and, scowling, tossed the derringer onto the desk.

If Glennon felt he had scored a victory, he had sense enough to know it was a small one. Calmly he dug a kitchen match out of that same open drawer, snapped its head into sputtering flame on his thumbnail and fired up the fresh cigar. With a cloud of blue smoke building in front of his face he dropped the gutted match into the cuspidor and, settling back, said in a conversational tone, "Can we talk business now?"

Vern Balance had almost forgotten their reason for coming back to this private office. As he looked at the other, Joe Glennon continued: "We're agreed I have three thousand that belongs to you. I wish I had the cash to pay you off and be rid of you, but I'm afraid that's out of the question—aside from what I need to operate, every dime is tied up in the building and stock and furnishings; and with the cattle business as it stands, there's no telling when there's hope of doing better. So, you see what it looks like."

"What?"

The fat man took the cigar from his lips, examined the way it was burning. "Why, we're back where we began: a partnership."

"Oh, no!" the other said sharply. "I'm not interested."

"Neither am I, frankly. Who needs a partner that accuses him of plotting murder? Under the circumstances, I'm being pretty damned generous. You might stop to consider"—and his cold stare pinned Balance's—"that you were careless enough—or dumb enough —to hand over that money without any strings at all. You've got no signatures, nothing on paper to prove I ever owed you a cent. Actually there's no reason I should have to give you anything."

This was true, and Balance felt his cheeks begin to heat up at the memory of such callow innocence. But his hand lifted to the gap in his coat and he said tightly, "I can give you a reason!"

The other stiffened; his eyes hardened to iron. "Don't threaten me!" he snapped. And then, in a slightly different tone: "I admit I'm a promoter. I've always been one, getting by on my wits—and a reputation for fair dealing. Once he loses that, a man like me might just as well fold his hand and drop out of the game. Which is the reason I have no intention of reneging on what I owe you, now."

In spite of himself, Balance found himself believing this. He dropped his hand and after a moment demanded grudgingly, "Just what did you have in mind?"

"What we first talked about, two years ago," the other said promptly. "A fifty-fifty proposition—right across the board. Actually, this sort of an enterprise needs two men to run it—there's more than one person alone can look after, almost twenty-four hours a day, and I've been wondering where I could find reliable help to share the job.

"So, we split the hours, and the responsibility, between us—and the profits, when there are any. What do you say? Is it a deal?"

When the other man only stared back at him, Glennon frowned and, turning his swivel chair, hauled a couple of account books out of their pigeonholes. "Here's the figures," he said. "You'll find all my correspondence and receipts and bills are filed, in good order. One thing I pride myself, I keep a clean set of records."

Vern Balance was scarcely listening. His own thoughts, just then, were heavy with the irony of things. Suddenly it seemed utterly unrealistic and foolish, to have imagined he could come here and force a showdown with someone like Joe Glennon. He had thought of himself as having grown ages older, bitterly wise and mature for the time he had spent behind the walls of Lansing Prison; suddenly, instead, he felt callow and helpless when confronted with a man who had proved entirely too tough a nut for him to crack.

If prison had matured him, he had needed this half hour to finish the educating process.

Angry and frustrated, he swore as he pushed up from the depths of the leather chair and strode the few short steps to the office doorway. But there he halted and turned back, to see the other man watching him intently through a blue haze of cigar smoke.

"Well?" Joe Glennon prompted him.

With a sour grimace Balance reached into his pocket and brought out a handful of change and one double eagle; the gold coin glinted in his palm as he showed it to the other man. "I'd *like* to tell you to go to hell," he said. "But this happens to be the tail end of my money. I've got nowhere to go, and no plans at all. I guess it has to be your proposition—or nothing!"

CHAPTER VI

The fat man showed his satisfaction, sweaty face gleaming in the lamplight. "I'm glad you see the sense of it. Somehow I've got a feeling we could make a winning combination. A drink, to seal the bargain?" he suggested. But when he took a bottle from one of the deep bottom drawers of the desk, a shake proved it to be empty. With a grunt of effort, Glennon hoisted himself to his feet and walked out of the office past Balance, to open the door to the main room. Balance watched him hold up the empty bottle, waggling it in signal to the bar. Afterwards he returned and set the bottle on the desk.

He looked at his new partner. "Well, first thing, it's obvious you need walking around money." From another drawer of the desk he removed a tin cash box, saying, "I guess we can spare you a hundred. You'll have to sign for it."

"All right." As Balance looked on it was counted out in coins and bills. He wrote a receipt on a slip of paper and signed his name, and saw this placed in the box which was then returned to the drawer. As he shoved the money in his pocket, he shook his head a little over the irony that found him in this bizarre arrangement with someone who might very well be his supreme personal enemy. Still, a man reduced to his last twenty-dollar gold piece had little room for choice. He was astonished that Glennon had offered the hundred, but he was asking no questions. It was a small enough return on the investment he had in this business.

Now the bartender came in bringing a fresh bottle and glasses. He set these on the desk and picked up the empty, raking Balance with a puzzled and suspicious glance; as he turned to leave, the latter stopped him. "Just a minute." And to Glennon: "If I'm a partner, there's going to be a change or two. I want this man fired!"

The bartender spun half around. With a quick frown, Glennon

exclaimed, "Nat Curry? But he's been with me since I opened. He's a good bartender."

"He's got sticky fingers," Balance replied coldly. "I was watching him this morning, while I waited for you. Two times out of three, drink money he collected over the bar missed the till box and ended up in his own pocket."

"That's a lie!" Nat Curry roared in injured fury.

"I know what I saw," Balance retorted, and told his partner, "I suggest you check the man's pockets. I'll wager you find them heavy with small change."

Curry shouted, "Nobody lays a hand on me!" and fell back a step, raising the bottle like a weapon. And Vern Balance slid his hand under his coat and brought out the gun.

The bartender's shoulders hunched on a caught breath as he saw it. The bottle, still raised, hung motionless as though he had checked the impulse to throw. Joe Glennon was looking from one man to the other, his eyes narrowed and his glance weighing them both in turn.

It settled on Balance. "Are you absolutely sure about this?" And when Balance, not deigning to repeat what he had already said, merely returned his look, the fat man's mouth drew down hard and he turned again to the bartender. "All right," he said. "You're through."

Curry's heavy jaw shot forward; rage kindled in his stare. "Just like that? Because of something this lying bastard tells you?"

"It isn't the first time," Glennon said bluntly, "I've had reports that made me wonder. And I've wondered why the receipts have always fallen short of what I'd of expected. Now I guess I know . . . Put that bottle down and get out."

The angry face changed, became sullen. "I got wages due me."

"I don't doubt," Vern Balance retorted, "you've more than collected them!"

For a moment, as the muddy eyes turned on him, he half expected the bottle to be flung straight at his head. But then Nat Curry set his lips in a hard line. He slammed the bottle down and a leather heel squealed as he strode savagely out of the office. A moment later they heard the barroom door slam, hard enough that the walls shook and a dingy print above the desk swung slightly on its nail.

Vern Balance put the gun away.

His new partner swore. "Shows you what I mean," Glennon said. "One man just can't keep an eye on everything. You see, you're already contributing to the partnership." He picked up the full bottle Curry had brought in. "Now, how about that drink?"

"If you don't mind," Balance said, "I think I'll pass."

He expected Glennon was going to take offense. The other merely gave him a sharp look and a shrug, saying, "If that's how you want it." Let him think what he liked. Balance saw no need to explain the oath he had taken.

He watched as Glennon pushed the cork from the bottle with a broad thumb, poured a scant two fingers. The fat man tasted the liquor judiciously, worked it over his tongue, and nodded to himself. "No better stock, any place in Ellsworth." He set his glass aside, picked up the derringer and without comment returned it to its drawer. "You do what you like," he said roughly. "I got to get back on the job."

And he was gone, leaving the bottle on the desk. Vern Balance picked it up, looked at the label—a good brand—and put it down again, satisfied to see that he felt no real desire. Idly he opened one of the account books Glennon had set out for his inspection; but after leafing through a few of the stiff pages, covered with the man's surprisingly neat, copperplate writing, he flipped it shut again, not even pretending to understand such things. He stood frowning at the darkened window, where full night had settled now, and asked himself what he thought he was doing here.

The irony of things was like a strong taste in his mouth. Two years ago, half ownership in an establishment like this one had been nearly the limit of his ambitions. Now it was very far from anything he wanted. It stood for a phase of his life he'd thought to put behind him.

But the hundred dollars in his pocket was real, reminding him that just now he had very few options. In his gambling days he had learned to play the hand that was dealt him. If the one strong card he had showing was the three thousand Joe Glennon owed him, then it was only common sense that he do what he could toward protecting his investment.

Still, a man liked to feel that he made his own choices. Balance was not in a particularly good mood as he followed his new partner out into the main room of the Oriental Palace.

Nat Curry seemed already to have left, as he'd been ordered; Joe Glennon was talking to the remaining bartender and Balance was starting forward to join them when Ben and Billy Thompson came in through the street door, with Cad Pierce and Neil Kane following. Billy was drunk. He lurched as he waded into the crowd, his brother's hand against a shoulder to steer him, and his coat sagging under the weight of a square gin bottle shoved in one pocket. He jostled someone; the man turned in angry protest, saw who it was and hastily stepped aside to give room.

Kane and Pierce found places at the bar, but Ben Thompson saw a vacant table and made for it. There Billy half fell into a chair, dropping his forearms heavily onto the baize top. As Ben pulled out a chair for himself, Vern Balance walked over.

"What did the judge say, Ben?"

"He was out of town," the Texan answered shortly. "Clerk set the hearing for next Tuesday."

Balance took a seat at the table. "Any idea what will happen?"

The other shrugged. "A twenty-dollar fine is about as far as he dares go. But that ain't the point," Ben said with sullen fury. "That sonofabitch Morco! Billy wasn't making any trouble—he wasn't doing a damn' thing!"

Mention of his enemy seemed to break through the fog in Billy's skull. He lifted his head with a wobbly effort, as though searching; his eyes were glazed and out of focus, and there was spittle at one corner of his slack mouth.

His brother observed him for a moment, then turned again to Balance. "I have to thank you," he said gruffly, "for stepping in." Balance acknowledged this with a bare nod, and Ben continued, "Another minute and it could have been murder—and the bastard would have got away with it! These goddam Kansas towns think they can treat a Texan like dirt! They rob him blind, with bad whiskey and crooked games, and if he dares make a fuss they turn loose an animal like Happy Jack Morco on him . . . or a murderer like Hickok!"

As he spoke that hated name, Ben Thompson had a look that made Balance repress a shudder. He knew about Thompson and Wild Bill Hickok: Phil Coe had been the Texan's best friend, as well as his partner in the Bull's Head. Balance had heard that when he got word of Coe's shooting, Ben had wept shamelessly and it was only the fact he was laid up with a hurt leg, broken in an accident in Kansas City, that kept him from setting out after revenge. Since that time, rumor had it Wild Bill was keeping discreetly out of his way—and no one that Vern Balance knew would give odds, either way, as to the outcome if the two should ever meet. Their reputations were that closely matched.

Billy had subsided again into drunken stupor, staring bleary-eyed at the table in front of him. Ben reached and pulled the half-empty gin bottle from his brother's coat pocket; he thumbed the cork, sniffed its contents, and then took a drag from the neck of the bottle and made a face.

"I don't know who sold him this stuff, but it's terrible! You can see, Ellsworth is Abilene all over again—they just never learn. Except for us, they'd be nothing. And if they ain't careful, the mood these men are in—with this damned heat, and their pockets empty, and the police pushing them around—the Texans might just naturally take their town away from them, one of these days, and tear the place to pieces!"

Frowning, Vern Balance said, "It can't all be that bad."

"Well, at least you can buy a decent drink here at Glennon's. On the other hand, there's not a place in town that's equipped to let a man sit down to enjoy an honest game. If he's fool enough to try that gambling hall out at Nauchville"—Balance guessed that was the red light district, east of the city limits—"he'll get knocked down and rolled for his winnings, almost before he's out the door."

Balance said, "You spoke this afternoon about starting a place of your own."

"I said I'd *like* to," the other corrected him. "Hell, I haven't got the capital. Nothing but a stickpin worth about two hundred dollars —not even enough to bankroll me, sitting in on a decent game." His tone was bitter. "Everything I had went into the Bull's Head—and when Phil was shot, the good people of Abilene managed to see to it I never got a dime of my investment back."

"Something might be worked out, though."

Thompson eyed him sharply. "What does that mean?"

Glancing toward the bar, Balance saw Glennon looking their way; he caught the man's eye, signaled to him. Turning back to the Texan he explained: "I hadn't mentioned it yet, but I've just gone in with Joe Glennon for a half interest."

"Oh? Somehow I got the impression, this morning, you wanted nothing more to do with the things that go on in a place like this."

"You might say I lost my personal taste for it," Balance said. "I don't expect other men to live by my standards." Glennon came up to the table, then. He nodded to Ben Thompson, flicked the drunken Billy with a distasteful glance. He looked at Balance, his eyes questioning; and the latter indicated a chair. "Sit down, Joe. An idea I want to try on you . . ."

The barrel chair creaked as the big man eased his weight into it. Briefly, Vern Balance repeated what Thompson had been saying. "If a man wants to gamble, it does seem he could be provided a place for doing it with some degree of dignity. It just occurred to me, it shouldn't be too much of a job to partition and convert some of that storage space into card rooms. Put in monte, faro—whatever the boys want. With Ben Thompson running the games—"

"Nothing doing!" the Texan broke in sharply. "I've never yet worked as anybody's house man. I'm not starting now."

"That's not what I had in mind. You'd run them to suit yourself; the house would merely supply the space and equipment, in return for a percentage. And we'd bankroll you at first, while you're getting started."

Put in those terms, Ben Thompson appeared to find the idea intriguing; he ran the ball of a thumb across his mustache while he thought it over. But Joe Glennon was scowling and he said heavily, "I dunno. That could be a heavy investment—and what do *we* get out of it? There's no big money floating around."

"Not at present," Balance agreed. "But that could change the moment the market breaks—and when it does we would have the edge, because every Texan knows that any game Ben Thompson runs is on the square. We'd get the cream."

His partner was forced to admit, "I see that . . ."

Vern Balance went on: "Certain rules, though, I have to insist on: There's to be no guns allowed at the tables. And no known card-sharps! Any man caught cheating even once is to be thrown out—for good." He was looking directly at Glennon and he knew the point went home, from the way the sweaty creases bulging above the man's collar took on a dull flush. Unrelenting, he continued: "If some young idiot is to get himself set up for trouble, it will be somewhere else— not here, not while I have anything to do with it!"

Glennon's mouth had hardened and his black eyes burned with anger, but Balance had the satisfaction of seeing the other break gaze before his own. Ben Thompson, unaware of the duel of looks, was saying, "I'll guarantee you honest games, at least. Hell, these are my friends! The trouble at Abilene was, Hickok owned an interest in the Alamo and he didn't like the Bull's Head taking business away— the Texans knew well enough where they could get an honest break. Hickok used every dirty trick to get us closed down, and when nothing else worked he turned to murder!"

Balance had heard several versions of the Abilene affair and he was not much concerned with it now. Instead he asked, "Is it a deal, then?"

"Give me a place to run my games," Thompson said, "and I'll get you business. I can promise you that."

"It's up to Joe, then."

Glennon, still scowling, took the cigar from his mouth and examined the fuming end of it. "Looks like you got it all arranged between you," he said heavily. He shrugged. "Well, hell! Go ahead."

The cigar was shoved again into the corner of his mouth and in an instant he was smiling again. "Sure—why not? We want the Palace to be the best place in town. Some high-money games in the back could give it class." He slapped both palms against the tabletop, leaned forward on them as he prepared to hoist his considerable bulk out of the chair. He looked at Billy Thompson.

"If he's going to be sick," he grunted, "I wish you'd get him outside. I don't want him doing it all over my table!" And with that he was on his feet and gone again, mingling with the crowd.

Vern Balance thought Ben Thompson might be angry, but there was nothing in his face to indicate it. The Texan was studying his brother, who had sunk deeper with his head now almost on the table and only his arms propping him. He did look sick, Balance thought; and Ben, scraping his chair back, said gruffly, "I'll take him home."

"It's been a long day for me," Balance said. "I could use some sleep, myself."

Billy's sweat-stained hat had fallen to the floor; Ben got it and jammed it on his head, and saying, "All right, kid. Let's go!" hooked a hand under his brother's arm and jacked him to his feet. Billy looked terrible, his eyes glazed and bloodshot and the hair plastered to the sweat that glistened on his face. He mumbled something incoherent but offered no resistance as Ben got him started for the door.

Vern Balance fell in on the other side, to lend a hand if needed and help shove a path clear. Men looked at them with varying expressions, but no one got in their way—and no one laughed.

Nightfall and darkness brought no end to the Kansas heat; it lay, dead and unstirring, upon the dark plaza. Emerging from the saloon, Balance asked, "Where are the two of you staying?"

"The Grand Central," Ben Thompson said, naming the new brick hotel on North Main, beyond the plaza and the railroad tracks.

"I'll walk over with you."

It took both of them to maneuver Billy across the uneven ground that was pitch black except for the white stars overhead, a scattered gleam of lamps in the depot and in buildings that lined the wide street, and a single lantern burning on a pole alongside the tracks. Billy kept lurching and stumbling over his own feet, and would have fallen without a tight grip on each arm. When they were halfway across, he all at once shuddered and with a horrible retching shout doubled over and brought up the foul stuff he had been drinking. They waited patiently until he was finished, and hanging limp and spent and evil-smelling between them; then Ben said dryly, "That's good! I was wondering when we'd get it over with."

Distasteful as he found this, Balance could remember occasions when he'd done as badly and he said nothing. Ben must have guessed at the run of his thoughts, however; standing there in the middle of the dark plaza, with the limp figure propped between them, he said soberly, "I wonder at times what's going to become of Billy. He's getting too old for this. He's mean, and he's wild—more than I can handle sometimes."

Vern Balance said, "What's going to become of any of us, Ben?"

There was a silence before the other answered. "Maybe you think I don't ask myself that . . . Where you from?"

"Indiana."

"Would you guess I was born in England? I'm a long way from there! Thirty years old, with a wife and son waiting back in Texas. And here I stand, with empty pockets, in a stinking little town that I got no more use for than it has for me. Ain't much to show, is it? I got no idea at all where I'm going—and you better start thinking, because you ain't but a step or two behind me!"

"I'm working on it," Vern Balance said—a bit lamely, because he could think of no better answer. He was frankly astonished to find himself taken into this man's confidence, but perhaps Ben Thompson was in a low mood—homesick for his wife and child, discouraged about his brother or the formlessness of his own life. Any man could be overtaken by things and feel the need for a moment's communication.

Whatever it was, the mood seemed to have passed. Balance waited but that was the end of it. Ben grunted something and they started on toward the lights of the hotel, guiding Billy's stumbling footsteps over the uneven ground.

Voiding the contents of his stomach appeared to have helped Billy considerably and he was managing fairly well by the time they reached the Grand Central. The hotel, east of the intersection of Lincoln and North Main, was newer and if anything more elegant than the Drovers Cottage: a solid brick structure with, surprising enough, a stretch of limestone sidewalk in front of it: "The only one this side of Kansas City, they tell me," Ben Thompson commented dryly when the other man remarked about it. "This town really thinks it's going to amount to something."

Standing in the spill of light from the hotel's front windows, Balance asked, "Can you get him to his room all right?"

"We'll manage," the other said gruffly. A brief exchange of good nights, and Balance turned and left them.

CHAPTER VII

Tired, and yet oddly restless and at loose ends, dissatisfied with the turn his arrival in Ellsworth had taken, he took out his last remaining stogie and fired it up. Across the dark plaza, the line of saloons along South Main poured their raucous hubbub into the Kansas night. Nearer at hand things were quieter; the town's more sedate stores and business houses, here on the north side, were closed for the night and showed light only in the windows of upper stories, which apparently served as homes for some of the merchants and their families. A lantern glowed in the cavernous entrance to a livery stable. Vern Balance dragged deeply at the cheap cigar, tossed the dead match aside, and started on the long diagonal across the plaza to his own room in the Drovers Cottage.

He paused once, wondering if he had caught a sound of footsteps grinding in right-of-way cinders somewhere ahead of him. If he had, it was not repeated and he could see no movement in the vague shadows. He moved on, crossing the tracks near the dark bulk of an empty boxcar sitting on the switch, and then cutting between this and the dimly lit railway station whose roofline cut a long silhouette against the stars. He could hear nothing now except his own footsteps, and the constant background of noise from the busy saloons across the plaza.

And then he rounded the high loading platform that flanked the depot's west end, and someone leaped at him from a hiding place beneath it. A mugger, he thought in the half second while he fell back before the attack—someone after whatever he could find in his victim's pocket. But then a glimmer of light from the depot's dusty windows showed him the face of the bartender, Nat Curry, and glinted off the metal rod he lifted to strike.

It was a crowbar, probably picked up along the tracks—an ugly weapon. There was no time to think about the gun in his shoulder holster. Balance scarcely got a protecting arm raised before the attacker was on him, in a silent rush. He deflected the downward blow aimed at bashing in his skull; then that other body slammed hard against him, and he lost the stogie and a grunt of exploding breath.

The man was bigger and heavier, and the collision nearly bowled him over. Keenly aware of the threat from that crowbar, Balance kept his left arm high in an effort to locate and trap the fist that held it. With his right, he swung a blow against his assailant's face that was dimly visible before him. He felt his knuckles hit, heard the man curse with pain. Curry was driven back but grabbed at his victim's clothing; locked in combat, they went reeling along the foot of the platform, colliding with the posts that supported it.

Balance was still grappling frantically for a hold on the crowbar. He missed; the man's arm slipped from his grasp and the metal bar descended, grazing the side of his skull, knocking the hat from his head, and striking his shoulder with a crushing force that turned the whole arm instantly numb. He heard himself cry out with the agony of it. But as he stumbled away from his attacker he had presence of mind to send his right hand groping at the opening of his coat. He found the clip holster, closed on the butt of the gun and dragged it forth—and then his elbow struck against a platform support with force enough to jar the weapon from his grasp. It made a blur of reflected light and went off, startlingly, when it hit the ground.

He glimpsed his attacker, in silhouette against the brief flash of light, with the crowbar lifting again to chop down at him. A little dazed, Balance tried to jerk aside but the piling at his back stopped him. A second later there was the clang of metal striking wood; he realized the crowbar had collided with the edge of the platform just inches above his head. Hardly thinking, he drove forward and his lowered head rammed into the bigger man's chest. Breath gusted directly in his ear. His left arm was still crippled; twisting, then, he reached with his right and was able to clamp a hold on the wrist that held the iron. He jerked, and levered Curry backwards off his feet, and dumped him heavily.

The crowbar dropped; Balance leaned and got it and flung it end over end, ringing across the ground. A quick search discovered his gun, lying where it had fallen, and he scooped it up, knelt and pressed the muzzle against his assailant's ear. The man had been making noises and threshing about; at its touch he went still.

Balance said roughly, "That's better!" and with his free hand searched him for a weapon but found none. Working to settle his breathing, he got to his feet.

Suddenly they were not alone. That gun going off was bringing men on the run; now someone came out of the depot carrying a lantern and, standing on the loading dock, held the lantern high so that it cast a swaying circle of yellow light over the scene below.

It showed Balance the glimmer of a metal badge, as he turned to face the ones who were closing in on him.

Morco again, he supposed resignedly. But then he made out the weak-jawed features and recognized the one called Brocky Jack Norton, whom he remembered from Abilene and who he had been told was now Ellsworth's marshal, and Morco's boss. With a half dozen other faces catching the glow of the lantern, the lawman confronted Balance and demanded officiously, "What's going on here? What happened?" In the next breath he added, "Oh—so it's you! Deputy Morco told me about you being in town and making trouble. What is it now?"

"If you really want to know," Balance told him coldly, "this fellow tried to brain me with a crowbar. Joe Glennon fired him from his job at the Palace, when I caught him cheating on the till. It was his way of getting back at me." He added: "You can check with Glennon if you want."

Balance expected Curry to put up a hot denial, but the man seemed to have had the fight knocked out of him; he stood panting a little, guiltily silent. The marshal scowled at him. "There's a couple trains out of here tomorrow," Norton told the man bruskly, "going either direction. You better make up your mind which one you want to take." Getting no answer, he looked again at Balance. He seemed to be trying, slow-wittedly, to get things sorted out. "Who was it got shot?" he demanded.

"Nobody," Vern Balance explained patiently. "The gun went off by accident. The real wonder is, I didn't have my skull bashed in."

Norton rubbed a hand across his mouth. He looked at the weapon in Balance's fist and frowned, shaking his head. "We can't have no gunplay within the city limits. There's an ordinance . . ."

"Yes, I heard all about the ordinance," Balance interrupted. "Just the same, I got a gun—and I'll carry it as long as I need it to protect myself. You can tell Happy Jack Morco I said so."

The marshal didn't like this. "I ain't sure we want *your* kind around here, either. I ain't forgetting the trouble you caused, back in Abilene."

"This isn't Abilene!" the other retorted. "I'm here on legitimate business. I don't want trouble and I'm not looking for it."

He waited defiantly for an answer, and there was a restless stir and shuffling of feet among the straggle of onlookers. When Norton seemed to find nothing to say, Balance nodded and turned, sliding his gun into the holster. He leaned for his hat, brushed it against a leg. And, straightening, found Nat Curry directly in his path.

He gave the man a cold, searching look, and after a moment the other ducked his head and stepped aside. Drawing on the hat, then, Vern Balance deliberately put his back to the group and walked away toward the lights of the Drovers Cottage.

He was furious, and his arm ached like the devil.

By morning the arm still bothered him a little, as he stood before the mirror in his room shaving with lukewarm water from the pitcher. Though it was early yet, the air that came through his window already held a shriveling heat and above the plaza the sky was like brass. Balance was in a poor mood, and when a knock sounded on his door he looked for a moment at the gun and holster lying on the chair beside the bed. But when the knock came again he shrugged, put down his razor and wiped the last of the lather from his face. Crossing the room, he dropped his towel casually on the chair, so that it covered the revolver; he opened the door and was surprised to see his caller was Jim Gore, the owner of the Drovers Cottage.

There was no greeting. The hotelman said, "Don't let me interfere, but I'd like to talk to you a minute." Balance nodded and stepped back, opening the door for his landlord to enter and then closing it again. Gore took in the room with a proprietary glance. "Everything comfortable?" he asked pleasantly.

"All but the heat. But I guess you can't do anything about that."

"Only wish I could!" Gore was a man about the same age as his wife, running a little to paunch, with a shrewd businessman's eye and a blunt, no-nonsense attitude that Balance had always liked about him. He said, "It looks like another scorcher. You keep hoping it will at least cool off at night; but it just seems to come back at you out of the walls and the ceilings, and the next morning is hotter than the one before . . . How's the Cottage look to you?"

Balance had returned to the commode, where he cleaned his razor and folded its blade into the handle. "Hasn't changed a bit," he said. "I keep thinking I should look out the window and see Joe McCoy's stockyards in Abilene."

Jim Gore chuckled. "The town paid me a four-thousand dollar subsidy if I'd have a hotel up and ready for the opening of the season, last year. I didn't tell them how I planned to do it. As it turned out I made a nice profit on the deal—and Ellsworth got them a first-class hotel, if I do say so. No one's complaining."

He dropped into the room's only rocker, mopping his face with a handkerchief. Balance was using the towel he'd taken off the chair by the bed; if Gore saw the gun it had covered, he made no comment, nor did he choose to say anything about the place where his guest had been for the past two years. Instead he said, with blunt directness, "I talked to our marshal, about the trouble you had last night with that Nat Curry. He'd been listening to Happy Jack Morco and was all primed to haul you in, after all—for assault and disturbing the peace.

"But I was able to tell him about Curry. The man worked a few days for me, down in the bar; he was totally unreliable and I had to let him go. Getting into the till is just what I'd expect of him—and then, trying to even things with the one who caught him at it. Anyway," Jim Gore concluded, "Curry's down at the depot now, with his bag packed and his ticket bought for the morning westbound; so, you've seen the last of *him*. And I don't think Norton will be bothering you any more about it either. I thought you'd like to know."

Balance said, "I'm obliged." He tossed the towel aside and reached for his shirt. Getting into it he added dryly, "I can't say I think much of your choice of a marshal, though—and even less of that deputy of his, that Morco. The fellow's obviously a thug. I can't imagine what your city council was thinking, or whoever it was hired him. He doesn't belong on anybody's police force."

Frowning, Gore looked down at the hands spread upon his knees. "I can't disagree with you," he admitted. "But perhaps I should tell you: I'm on the city council!"

Balance stared at him. "Then why on earth—?"

"Believe me, I put up a real fight against hiring Happy Jack Morco," the other explained patiently, "but I was outvoted. It happened early in the season, when things looked like they might be getting out of hand. Some of the trail crews, hitting town, took to shooting things up—nobody hurt, just signboards and the like; but people got worried and it was voted to beef up the police force. Later, when things quieted down again, I talked the council around to getting rid of Happy Jack Morco—but when we tried it, the townspeople got up a petition and we had to hire him back.

"You have to understand that people here are afraid. There hasn't been a season yet without shootings; and this year, what with things the way they are, feelings are pretty tense."

Vern Balance had his shirt buttoned, the tails shoved into his trousers and the belt fastened. Now he leaned back against the bedframe, shaking his head. "Don't they know these Texas boys are proud—that they won't be lorded over by trash like Happy Jack Morco?"

Jim Gore shrugged. "They've got a notion that he's tough enough to keep the trail crews under control. That's all they're thinking about; and if that's how they want it, there's nothing I can do."

"What about the rest of your police?"

"You mean Ed Hogue and Jack DeLong. They're pretty much the same caliber, I'm afraid. Frankly, I don't think Norton's strong enough to keep his men in line—but they're all that's available.

"Maybe you can see," Gore pointed out, "I'm sort of caught in the middle. As a hotelman, I do my business with the drovers and naturally I want them and their crews to have a fair shake—Ellsworth is certainly in no position to kick them out, the way they've gone and done in Abilene. But the mayor is a real estate man, name of Miller, and the rest of the council is mostly people like him. All they can think about is keeping the lid on, and the Texans in their place. And like I say, they believe a tough police force will do it."

"If they knew the talk I've heard, in the few hours I've been here, they might think differently! They don't know it, but Happy Jack Morco's planting the seeds of trouble for them—and if they don't look out, they're apt to reap the harvest."

Gore shook his head. "I'd hate to see it happen. Ellsworth ain't a bad town, really. There's some mighty good people here, who could get hurt through no fault of their own. Cap Whitney—"

"The sheriff? I met him yesterday."

"A fine fellow—but being a county officer, his hands are tied where the town is concerned. And there's John Montgomery, his brother-in-law, that runs the newspaper—they married the Henry sisters, and a nicer family you wouldn't want to know . . ." Jim Gore slapped his hands on his knees, then, and came to his feet. "Well, I didn't come up here to spend the morning jawing. Just wanted to tell you about what I said to the marshal."

Balance nodded. "Thanks again for that, Jim."

But he had a feeling the other actually had something more on his mind. He waited, and sure enough, with a hand on the doorknob Gore faced him again. "What about Tess Spearman?" he demanded bluntly.

Face expressionless, Vern Balance turned the question back. "What about her?"

"I think you know!" Jim Gore looked suddenly angry. "It ain't just that the girl's been left with Lou and me, and that we're responsible. Truth is, we think as much of her as if she was our own—and if I believed you had some notion of taking it out on her, for what you've been through these last two years—"

Balance cut him off. "Forget it! I told your wife, and I'll say it to you: The last thing I want in the world, is to cause any more hurt to that family!"

They looked at one another, across the stillness of the sweltering hot room, with sounds of the street drifting through the open window. Then Gore's manner changed; the stiffness eased out of him and his hard expression melted. Nodding, he actually let a corner of his mouth quirk in a smile. "She's an attractive girl, isn't she? I couldn't blame you for being interested."

"I haven't said I'm interested," Vern Balance retorted. "I'd be a damned fool if I was! The minute she finds out who I am—"

"Yes, I see." Gore nodded slowly. "Bud Spearman was no great loss—for all I could see, he was on his way to becoming something not a hell of a lot better than that Billy Thompson. Still, where Clayt Spearman was concerned, the sun rose and set in that boy; and from one or two things the girl has let drop, it was quite a loss for her, too. Apparently that's why she was never told any details about what happened to her brother.

"A minute ago, I was all ready to say I'd tell her the truth, myself, rather than let you work into her confidence with an idea of doing something wrong. But maybe I jumped to false conclusions. If I did, and you really like that girl—then I can only say you've got a problem! The wife and me, though, we won't make things any worse by interfering. I dunno, I kind of think I can trust you."

"Thanks, Jim," Balance said soberly. "You can."

It looked as though the other man had finally got off his chest the thing he'd really come to talk about, and was at least partly satisfied with his answer. There were no more questions—no prying at all into his guest's plans, or his intentions here in Ellsworth. Jim Gore turned the knob and with a final nod was gone, closing the door after him.

Vern Balance was frowning thoughtfully as he went and picked up the shoulder harness and slipped into it. There was one thing he'd somehow lost sight of, in his commitment as half owner of the Oriental Palace: No longer would he be spending a few short hours in Ellsworth, as he'd planned, and then be gone again. In all probability, and whether he liked it or not, he would still be here when Clayt Spearman returned from his search for a buyer.

He thought of a meeting, and he thought of Tess; and already he felt a small, cold knot of apprehension.

CHAPTER VIII

He looked for her in the dining room while he had a late breakfast; seeing nothing of her, he found himself wondering how she passed her days. Alone in her room, he supposed—and hoped it had better ventilation than his own: When he left it for the street, the mounting heat was already turning the place into an oven.

The men Tess Spearman would encounter in the lobby and dining room and hallways of the Drovers Cottage were, of course, mostly Texas cattlemen and therefore of a type thoroughly familiar to her. Still, Vern Balance could imagine it was lonely for a young girl, by herself and so far from home. He felt a little sorry for her, and thought again how fortunate it was she had the Gores to look after her.

At nearly ten o'clock, he walked into the Oriental Palace, finding it darker but scarcely any cooler than the white blast of morning outside. There was only a scattering of trade. At his question the bartender on duty indicated the door at the rear of the long room and Balance walked back there, aware now of a sound of hammering and sawing from beyond the partition.

Considerable work had already been done there. Someone had cleaned out the trash and empty barrels and broken furniture, probably to dump them in the alley behind the saloon, and now two men were nailing in the first dividers for new partition walls, while a third marked saw lines for opening up a window. Joe Glennon, in shirt-sleeves and with a cigar fuming between his lips, was supervising the job. He gave Balance a curt nod, and at the latter's questioning look he shrugged and said, "Once a thing's decided on, I believe in getting on with it."

"So it appears . . ."

Glennon led the way into his office, where he eased his weight into the desk chair. "Thompson was in, earlier this morning, and we settled on the floor plan. We figured there's space for three rooms—fairly small, but adequate for an uninterrupted private game, which is what we're after." He picked up a sheet of paper and handed it to the other. "We also drew up a list of stuff we'll be needing to order out from Kansas City."

Balance read over the list, standing. "Looks like you're going all out."

"Might as well do a thing right." The chair creaked as Joe Glennon eased back comfortably, fingers laced across his vast middle. "Truth is, I been talking around—let out a few hints as to what we're doing; and I got a good reaction. Like I said last night, this can add tone to the place, get the right kind of people in here." He nodded at the paper. "I'm thinking I may add some carpets to that list."

"Carpets?"

"They shouldn't cost much. I told you, the rooms will be small. But we want them comfortable—a place where a drover or a commission man with money in his pocket will feel like spending an evening, sitting in a high stakes game. I'm thinking of clubs I've seen in St. Louis and Chicago: a high-class clientele, the best liquor, thousand-dollar antes . . ."

Looking at him, Vern Balance almost said, "Flying pretty high, don't you think?" But he recognized, with dry clarity, that that was the man's nature. He had sensed it during their talks at Abilene, and realized even then that, the more Joe Glennon talked, the less convincing he became. Probably it was the reason he was still talking, still promoting—scrounging for the money to invest in his grandiose dreams. You could see the truth, in the contrast between his talk and the Oriental Palace with its tawdry reality.

But there was no point in saying any of this, and Balance merely nodded and laid the list on the desk. Someone had dropped a nickel into the mechanical piano; the strident thump of drum and crash of cymbal came through the thin wall and he nodded to the sound. "You know you may have to get rid of that thing."

Glennon bristled instantly. "Like hell! It cost me a hundred dollars, in Kansas City!"

"A man with a thousand in the pot doesn't want a brass band at his ear while he concentrates. Maybe, if you moved it against another wall, that would help muffle it. Otherwise, it can lose us business."

Scowling, the fat man said nothing; Balance thought he must recognize the sense of that and he didn't press it. Instead he asked, "Is Thompson around?"

"Went back to the hotel," Glennon answered shortly. "That brother of his was sleeping off a hangover. Ben said he had to get him on his feet, and pour enough coffee in him to get him to court by eleven."

Balance had forgotten that Billy had a hearing scheduled. On an impulse he asked, "Where's it held? The county courthouse?"

"No, this is the police court—in the council room over Larkin's store, across the plaza."

"Thanks." And, seeing the curious look the other gave him: "After all, if I'm to be doing business in this town, I ought to have a look at the way the legal machinery operates . . ."

The council room, above a flight of stairs that snaked up the outside wall of the drygoods store, was musty-smelling and breathlessly hot. For furnishings there were a table and chairs used by the members of the city government, backless benches for the handful of visitors. When Vern Balance entered, court was already in progress.

The police judge, a heavy man who had sagging jowls and a saddle of thinning black hair combed across his sweating scalp, sat at the table in a blue-striped shirt without a collar; beside him his clerk—dried-up, birdlike, with a tic under one eye—made notes. The judge's voice droned in the heated stillness and the newcomer, entering, heard him delivering a lecture to the two men before him.

Vern Balance halted at the door, in cold astonishment.

Gamblers and prostitutes, the judge was saying, were a plague that rotted the fiber of a community like Ellsworth. He switched metaphors: They were vermin—rather, they were vultures who fed on the lifeblood of the cattle trade and brought with them chaos and civil disturbance. If he could, he would use the law to rid the town completely of such parasites. And so the voice droned on, without a break, in the stillness. At one side, by an open window, Happy Jack Morco leaned against the wall with arms folded and the police badge on his vest front gleaming faintly; his teeth showed in a grin of pleasure and his eyes never left the pair who received the judge's tongue-lashing.

Billy Thompson looked too hungover to have much idea of what was being said; but the partial view Balance had of Ben's face showed it pale, and set with a contained anger. Now, as the judge paused for breath, Ben Thompson answered him crisply. "Your Honor, what a Texas cowhand wants to do with his time and his money, after three months on the trail, should be his own business. What's more, it's beside the point. My brother isn't here at the moment to answer for being a professional gambler. He's charged with carrying a weapon, he pleads guilty, and he's ready to pay his fine. Now, let's get on with it!"

He made no effort to keep disrespect out of his voice. He had solid legal ground under him; after a brief contest of stares, it was the judge who settled back with an angry shrug of his shoulders. "Twenty dollars," he snapped. "I'd make it more if I could. I promise you, if I see him in here again, on a similar charge—next time, I will!"

Ben was already taking out a leather wallet. He counted the amount in small bills, dropped them wordlessly on the table, waited for the receipt which the clerk's scratching pen filled in. Morco had come forward and was waiting with outstretched palm for his fee; the clerk put two dollars in it, and Morco's grin was openly mocking as his fingers closed on Ben Thompson's money.

"Next case!" the judge said bruskly.

Billy, who had not uttered a word up till now, suddenly stirred himself. "What about my gun?"

It lay on the table, the evidence in the case against him. The clerk gave the weapon a push and Billy had started to reach for it, when the elder Thompson halted him.

"One minute," said Ben. He looked directly at Morco. "Seems to me, it would only be good manners if our deputy marshal was to pick up that gun and hand it to him."

Balance, who had had no idea what was coming, could hardly believe the audacity of it. He saw Morco's whole face turn slowly red. As the Texan's words hung upon the stillness, the judge stiffened in his chair. "Now, hold on here!"

Ben Thompson simply ignored him, not moving his stare from Happy Jack Morco's.

He had been smart enough not to wear a weapon into the courtroom; yet, even so, unarmed as he was there was a potent threat about the man from Texas—partly it lay in the force of his stare, partly in the reputation that hung about him like a cloud. Even the judge seemed to recognize this, and after his one protest he fell silent. The whole weight of the room's attention lay on Happy Jack Morco.

During a terrible moment, while he faced the humiliating choices offered him, Morco changed color again—from angry red to deathly pallor. Finally, with a hand that shook from the hatred in him, he seized the weapon from the table and extended it butt first to Billy Thompson. The latter merely stared at it, and Balance wondered if he even understood what was happening. But then Billy's chest swelled and he threw a triumphant stare around him. He said, loudly, "So this is the tough killer that thought he had the town buffaloed!"

Ben cut him off, in a tone of disgust. "Just shut up—and take it!" And when Billy, with a shrug, had accepted the gun from Morco's hand and shoved it into his empty holster: "Now let's get out of here."

The judge found his voice, then. "If he's still wearing that gun an hour from now, I'll have him arrested again!"

Already turning Billy toward the door, Ben answered across a shoulder: "He won't." And then he was herding his brother along the aisle, past the few staring spectators on the benches.

Billy still looked physically ill, and unsteady on his legs. As they reached the door where Vern Balance waited, the latter saw him stumble and he put out a hand, offering to help; but Ben shot him a glance and a quick shake of the head. Balance let the hand fall and stood aside, making room to let them pass. Afterward, following outside, he stood on the landing and watched them maneuver the steep flight of wooden steps to the ground, Billy leaning heavily on the rail. They turned in the direction of the Grand Central Hotel.

As they passed from view beneath the store's awning, someone came through the door behind Balance and he looked quickly around.

The man was about his own age, bareheaded and bespectacled, with a row of sharpened pencils in one pocket of his waistcoat and a notebook in his hand. Balance had noticed him, sitting on one of the benches at the back of the courtroom and industriously scribbling in the book. He had a direct look and a manner that suggested he did not waste time on formalities.

He said, "I'd like to have a word with you. Are you Vern Balance?"

"That's my name."

"I'm John Montgomery. I edit the Ellsworth *Reporter*."

Balance nodded. He remembered seeing the tiny box of a newspaper office, next door to the Grand Central; he remembered too what Jim Gore had told him, about the editor being Sheriff Whitney's brother-in-law.

Montgomery answered the question in his look. "Cap was talking about you. He says you can tell me what happened yesterday, between Morco and the Thompsons."

"He knows as much as I do. He was there."

"But not until it was nearly over. He tells me there was shooting."

"There was one shot," Balance corrected him. Standing there at the head of the steps with the plaza below them baking in noonday sunlight, he described the incident briefly, and the ineffectual blow from the younger Thompson's fist. "Billy was too drunk to be dangerous. It looked to me that Morco was spoiling for trouble."

The other said, "You thought he actually intended to kill Thompson?"

"It looked to me he was too far out of control to know, himself." Balance added, "You mean to quote me in your paper?"

"Would you rather I didn't?"

"Doesn't make much difference. My opinion won't come as any news to Morco."

Montgomery raised an eyebrow. He said dryly, "From what you say, you don't seem to think much of our deputy marshal."

"I figure Ellsworth probably has what it wants."

"Maybe not," the newspaperman said quickly. "Maybe there are enough people with heads on their shoulders, that sooner or later the town will have to wake up to what its police force is doing."

Balance shrugged; he was wholly skeptical. "Maybe," he said.

They fell abruptly silent as Jack Morco came out upon the landing. He halted and shot a quick, scowling look at the pair of them, as though somehow knowing he was the subject of their talk. There was rank hostility in the stare he gave Balance. But he said nothing; his mouth set hard and he swung past them and went down the steps, at a curious slack-kneed prowl, his boots thumping heavy echoes from the wooden treads.

They stood and watched him go.

CHAPTER IX

After three days, the workmen had largely completed their chores on the new gambling rooms behind the Oriental Palace. Partitions were in, doors hung, windows installed; a pleasant mingling of smells —new paint and pine shavings—had taken the place of the musty storeroom odors. Vern Balance found the work interesting and had taken charge of overseeing the job during the short time it took. But now it was finished, waiting for the furnishings and supplies to arrive on the cars from Kansas City; and Balance found himself bored and restless, with nothing useful to do.

He was in this mood as he entered the lobby of the Drovers Cottage, finding it pleasantly dim after the glare of sun on street dust and clapboard building fronts. The constant prairie wind that breathed at the open windows carried the smells of dust and of the sun-scorched miles over which it had traveled; though it kept the air circulating, it was as dry and searing as the blast from an oven.

The lobby for once was nearly deserted—no one behind the desk, silence except for the murmur of voices beyond the doorway to the bar. A heavy-bodied man sat like a lump at one end of a stiff horsehair sofa, with his booted legs apart and a week-old copy of the *Reporter* spread before his face. A woman was at a corner table by a window, writing a letter. As Balance looked at her, something caused her to glance up; it was Tess Spearman. Their eyes met, and she smiled as though delighted to see someone she knew.

It was the first time they had exchanged a word since their dinner together. Crossing the carpet to her, Vern Balance took off his hat as he asked, "Is this where you spend your time, these days?"

She had laid down her pen. "It gets terribly warm in my room during the middle of the day." She smiled as she said it, but to Balance she looked wilted, badly used by the containing heat and the confinement. After all she was, he remembered, a ranch girl.

"You can't be having much fun—just waiting around for your father."

Tess said, "I've thought once or twice of getting out to take a walk, but Mrs. Gore won't let me—she says it's not proper, and in a strange town like this one I suppose she's right. And, of course, she and her husband are both much too busy, to have time for me . . ."

"As for the town," Vern Balance said, with a gesture toward the window and the empty plaza lying baking in the sun, "you can see about all there is to it from here." Twenty minutes ago there had been the usual flurry of excitement when the afternoon train, east-bound, pulled through—stopping briefly before it rolled on again, shaking the flimsy buildings with the pound of its drive wheels and tanging the heated air with the smoke from its diamond stack. Now Ellsworth was sunk again in torpor.

The door to the office, behind the desk, opened and Lou Gore appeared with a fistful of mail which she began sorting into the pigeonholes on the wall. On a sudden decision, Balance excused himself and walked over there.

He was certain she had noticed him talking to the girl, but her face was expressionless as she turned. Balance came directly to the point. "That young lady," he said bluntly, "is dying of boredom, and it's not right. She should get out."

"I won't dispute that," the woman said, looking at him, her hands bristling with envelopes. "But what about it?"

"I have an hour to spare. I was thinking I could rent a rig and take her for a little ride in the country. That is," he added pointedly, "if you're willing to risk it."

Frowning, Lou Gore looked at the letters she was holding. She didn't answer, while she sorted out a couple of the envelopes, tapped them on the counter to square their edges, and placed them in one of the compartments of the rack. Then she turned back and her look met Balance's.

She said—reluctantly, he thought—"My Jim says you're to be trusted. All right. I don't particularly like it, but this once I'll trust you. You said an hour. Don't make it a minute longer."

"An hour, it is," Vern Balance agreed.

He was repaid for his trouble when he told Tess Spearman the news. She was as delighted as a child. "Could we *really?*" she exclaimed, jumping to her feet; and then, hesitating: "Are you sure you have the time to bother?"

"I don't know what makes you think it's a bother," he said, smiling. "You get ready. I have to step across the plaza to Nagle's, and see about renting us an outfit."

"I won't keep you waiting." She was already hurrying toward the stairs.

When he returned over the plaza, tooling a black-topped buggy with a roan mare between the shafts, Tess was watching for him and came quickly out upon the porch as he brought the rig to a halt. She was dressed as he had first seen her, that day in the upper corridor of the hotel, and she had done her hair up beneath a pert hat with a brim that would shield her face from the fierce beat of the sun. She carried a brown paper bundle tied with string; as Balance stepped down to help her into the buggy she explained: "Mrs. Gore had the kitchen put us up some sandwiches. I thought that was sweet of her."

"She's a goodhearted woman," Vern Balance agreed. "Even if she doesn't see a great deal in *me.*" He got in and took the reins; Tess settled her skirt about her, placing the bundle in her lap. After they were in motion, he admitted, "I never asked if you wouldn't rather I'd rent a couple of saddle horses. I guess I took it for granted you didn't have any riding clothes with you. Besides"—and he smiled ruefully—"I'm not really all that much of a horseman. I didn't feel like showing myself up, in front of someone who was raised on a ranch!"

"This is fine," she assured him. "Just anything for fresh air, and a change of scenery . . ."

They took the road west from town, following the rails past the stockyard and shipping pens which, being no more than half filled with cattle, showed the depressed state of the market—now, in the heart of summer, in what should be the very midst of the shipping season. Then all this was behind them, and they had the shallow river on their left with its lining of cottonwood and willows, and about them the swells of rolling prairie, and the clean smells of sun-scorched grass on the warm wind that quartered against them under the buggy's shading top. The road looped away beneath the spinning wheels and the hoofs of the mare, ambling along at the comfortable gait Balance set for her.

In any direction they looked, it seemed, there were Texas cattle and the men who tended them.

Tess offered tentatively, "I think I told you, our trail camp is supposed to be somewhere north of here—four miles or so, I understood. There'll be riders I haven't seen since they left Texas, back in the spring."

Balance had thought of that and was prepared for it. "We only have an hour," he pointed out. "That doesn't give us enough time. Maybe, another day, Mrs. Gore will let us be gone longer."

"Maybe she will."

The girl seemed satisfied with that, and he was relieved. It was all too possible there would be men at that camp who knew him by sight, and who could betray his identity—something he wasn't yet ready for. Sooner or later, this girl was going to learn who he was; the wonder was that some hint—some overheard remark, perhaps, in the lobby of the Drovers Cottage—hadn't already given her the clue. But he certainly didn't mean for it to happen while he confronted a group of her father's hostile trail crew, with the girl completely unprepared for what she was about to hear.

His thoughts made him silent, and presently he was aware of her look resting on his face, in a troubled frown. She said suddenly, "You're a strange sort of man, you know. You've told me nothing at all about yourself—or what you're doing in Ellsworth. Of course, it's none of my business, either; but I'll admit I've been curious. I even asked Mrs. Gore about you."

"Oh?" A corner of his mouth quirked wryly. "And what did she say?"

"Not very much. But she did tell me you were some sort of a—gambler." From the way she spoke the word, Balance couldn't help but sense that the news had come as a disappointment.

He shrugged. "Every man in the state of Kansas is some sort of a gambler. The man who tries to farm this prairie land, or who starts a business in a town like Ellsworth . . . Your father gambles whenever he puts a herd on the trail, for a market that may not even exist by the time his cattle reaches it. But if you mean someone who follows the card tables—yes, I used to do that, when I was a few years younger. But I quit; and now I don't know exactly where I'm going, or what I want to do." He looked at her. "So if I don't talk much about myself, I suppose that's the reason: I'm not really sure who I am!"

She had listened solemnly. "I think I can understand that," she said. "And I really didn't mean to pry."

"You haven't," he assured her.

They rode awhile without talking, and then he reined left toward the riverbank. He fastened the anchorweight to the mare, and helped Tess down. They strolled awhile along the bank, watching the Smoky Hill slide past—shrunken with summer drought, the sun a shimmering smear reflected in its muddy current.

The trunk of a dead cottonwood, brought down in some hard prairie blow, made an inviting place to sit, with other trees overhead to shade them; Tess opened the package of sandwiches, and found also a jar of cold tea. They made a picnic of it, and Vern Balance could not remember a time he had enjoyed himself more than in this homely pleasure, with the girl for company—except for the unspoken truth that he felt like a wall between them, and that filled him all the more with guilt the longer he let it stand.

If he did not tell her himself, she must eventually learn the facts from some other source; and that would be far worse. More and more, as the moments slipped inexorably by, he began to sense that this was the time when he should speak if he ever intended to. But there were no words in his mind, until finally he decided an oblique approach was the only one that would actually bring him to the subject.

Into a little silence he said casually, "You come from a large family?"

She had been smiling slightly, as though at some thought of her own. The smile died and a frown pulled at her brow as she answered hesitatingly, staring into the sliding water. "Oh, no," she said. "In fact, there's only the two of us—Papa and me. Mama died when I was little. I just had the one brother—and now, he's gone too."

Looking at her, Balance said, "And you miss him . . ."

"Oh—dreadfully! We were very close, Bud and I." She explained:

"He was named for Papa, actually, but that's what everyone always called him. He was just enough older that I used to rely on him for everything; he'd be there whenever I was hurt, or needed comforting.

"But then Papa was injured in a riding accident, and had to throw responsibility onto Bud—I think, before he was quite old enough. You could see the change in him. He turned cocky, hard to get along with—for nearly everyone else, that is; not me. Where *I* was concerned, he never changed at all. I'm sure, now, that he was really frightened of the load that was being put on him, and trying hard to cover up."

"That can happen," Balance agreed.

She went on as though he hadn't spoken: "Then—it was just two years ago this spring—he left for Kansas with a trail herd and I never saw him again. They brought him home in a coffin that couldn't be opened. No one would ever tell me exactly what happened, but that didn't keep the men from talking. I managed to learn a little—I heard that Bud had been shot to death, at Abilene. By some gambler . . ."

Anything Vern Balance might have said just then would have been the wrong thing and he held his tongue, though he could feel a cold knot forming inside him as he listened to her words. "I guess you can see," Tess went on, "that I'm prejudiced against professional gamblers! I can't find any reason or excuse for them. That's why I admit I was upset when I heard that you were one. I'm—glad you aren't, any longer."

It took a tremendous effort to form words. "There sure doesn't appear that there's much chance you'd ever forgive the man who killed Bud Spearman. Your brother must have been one of the biggest things in your life."

"Whoever the man was," she admitted, and her voice was bitter, "I just hope I never have to come face to face with him, *that's* all!"

"Yes," Vern Balance said—a poor answer, but he was almost beyond speech. Abruptly he stood, unable to continue this. "I imagine," he said gruffly, "it's time we were leaving, if we intend to be back inside an hour . . ."

The girl looked at him strangely, but made no protest as she stood and brushed her skirt and let him lead her to the waiting buggy.

Neither spoke more than a few words during the return trip to the Drovers Cottage.

The shotgun was a handsome piece, English-made, with twin barrels and rimfire action; Ben Thompson said it had cost his friend Cad Pierce $150, and he had made Ben a present of it on a whim, knowing the latter took a good deal of pride in being of English birth. Ben had been keeping the gun in his room at the Grand Central, but this morning he had brought it over to the Oriental Palace, to lock it in a cabinet he'd had built in a corner of one of the new card rooms. He had no intention of letting trouble arise that might get out of hand; and he assured Balance that nothing in the world could cool off a hotheaded loser any quicker, than a look at the shining tubes of the shotgun pointed at his head.

Ben gave the barrels and handcrafted stock a swipe with the chamois and offered the weapon to Balance. It had a good heft to it —an efficient killing instrument, whether of men or of game. Balance suppressed a slight shudder as he handed the weapon back, and watched it put away in the cupboard. "A nice piece of firearm," he agreed laconically.

Morning sunlight slanted into the room, past maroon curtains at the window. The furnishings had arrived and been installed: a heavy walnut table and comfortable chairs for the players, a new brass lamp suspended above them, a couple of framed hunting prints on the walls—even the carpet underfoot that Joe Glennon had promised. In his enthusiasm, Glennon had spared no expense. Balance thought he really had some notion the Oriental Palace could be made over in the image of the club he still hoped one day to own, like those he had seen and envied in St. Louis and Chicago.

If so, it was a fantasy. Balance knew the cattle trade was going to prove as ephemeral, here in Ellsworth, as it had in Abilene. It would move west eventually, following the rails; and when it did the Oriental Palace would be left to die on the vine.

A carton stood on the table. As Balance dropped into one of the chairs Thompson split the box open with a swipe of his pocketknife, then upended it and poured out its contents—unopened packages of playing cards. He began working swiftly, checking each deck to make certain the seal had not been broken before stowing it back in the carton. He cast a look at the other man from beneath his brows and said presently, "You have a glum look this morning . . ."

Balance lifted a shoulder. The reaction from yesterday afternoon still weighed heavily on him—his inability to speak the truth to Tess Spearman, to unburden himself of the heavy weight of guilt in her brother's death. He knew perfectly well that his silence, during the ride back to town and until the moment when he deposited her at the Drovers Cottage, had betrayed to Tess that something was very wrong; just how wrong, she would understand soon enough, when she finally learned from someone else the thing he hadn't been able to tell her. And now even Ben Thompson—who was little more than a stranger—could read in him the sour aftermath.

He was certainly not going to discuss Tess Spearman with Thompson, or anyone else. He told the other man gruffly: "Just out of sorts, I guess."

"You've been out of sorts since you hit Ellsworth," Ben Thompson commented shrewdly. "I've still got an idea you're none too happy about the deal you've gone and got yourself involved in, with Glennon. But, a man usually makes what he can of what's thrown in his way. He doesn't have too much choice."

That was true enough, Balance reflected bleakly. You weren't often actually the designer of your own fate. Things happened, and though you could fight the tide you generally ended up going where it took you. But it wasn't a thing that anyone liked having to admit.

The one-armed oldster who served the Palace as a swamper shoved his head in the door, mop in hand. His voice held a note of alarm. "Morco's here," he said. "Wants to talk to somebody in charge."

Balance exchanged a look with Ben Thompson. "I guess that's me. I wonder what he's after."

"It won't be anything good . . ."

Happy Jack stood with an elbow on the bar, nursing a drink he probably had no intention of paying for. The hat was pushed well back from his bristling rooster's comb of stiff brown hair. The glass was in his left hand; he had his right thumb hooked into his belt, not far from the revolver handle jutting from its holster. When he heard

Vern Balance approaching, with Thompson behind him, the deputy marshal pivoted on the elbow and watched them come with a look of sinister expectation as a quiet fell over the room, over the usual morning crowd—they all seemed to know that something out-of-the-way was shaping up.

Vern Balance came to a stand, facing Morco. "Do you and I have business?" he asked bluntly, his voice implying that he doubted it.

Happy Jack took his time finishing his drink. His stare raked Balance, deliberately. "I understand you're the new owner of this place."

"Co-owner," Balance corrected him. "I'm partners with Joe Glennon."

"Same difference. I also understand you got gambling in your back rooms."

"There are card rooms, yes. We open them tonight."

"So I heard. And that's why I'm here: You ain't paid your fine yet. I've come to collect it."

Balance's eyes narrowed. "I know nothing about a fine."

"You should have asked your friend Thompson—he's been payin' *his*." Morco was enjoying himself. Very deliberately, he toyed with his whiskey glass, making circles with it on the bar. "We got a town ord'nance."

"Still another?" Balance said coldly.

"This one's aimed at undesirables. Whores and gamblers plyin' their various trades within the corp'rate limits of Ellsworth are declared a nuisance and charged ten dollars a month. The fine is double, for a person or establishment profiting from the activities of such undesirables. Now, I take it that includes you."

Vern Balance, staring at him, felt the heat begin to mount into his cheeks. There was no mistaking Morco's intent—it showed in the way he had phrased his statement, so as to place the other man in exactly the same category as a pimp or a madam. Happy Jack was watching him to see how he would take the insult. From the hush that had fallen upon the room, Balance knew everyone else was waiting too, with held breaths.

He turned to Ben Thompson. "How about this? Is he telling it straight?"

The Texan nodded with a sour expression. "I never thought to mention it. They call it a fine but it's just one more way to put the screws on us. The Palace will already have put up a hundred for a liquor-selling license. It didn't occur to me that this gambling tax would apply to us, as well."

Balance looked again at the lawman. "If it's on the books," he said coldly, "then I guess we'll have to pay. Twenty dollars, you said?"

"Per month," Morco reminded him.

He took a gold double eagle from his pocket and laid it on the bar. But when the policeman moved to take it Balance kept his hand on the coin. "First, I'll want a receipt."

Happy Jack Morco checked his reach, scowling. "A receipt," Vern Balance repeated. "You didn't think I'd hand over the money without getting one?" He looked at the bartender, who was watching as intently as all the others in the room. "Got any paper there? And a pencil?"

The man stirred himself, quickly rummaging under the counter to find the pad that was kept handy for an occasional bar tab. He placed this in front of Morco and laid a well-chewed pencil stub beside it. "Twenty dollars," Balance told the lawman, who eyed the pencil without picking it up. "Write it out, sign it, and date it."

Morco made no move to do so; the pencil might have been red hot, from the wary look he gave it. And then, as the moment stretched out, somewhere in the room there was a hoot of laughter and a voice said scornfully, "Hell! Everybody knows Happy Jack can't even write his own name!"

Another picked up the laughter, and another, and then still more. Morco's head jerked up and around, his face going brick red. Not hurrying, Vern Balance picked up his coin and pocketed it again; he said, "I guess I'll have to go in and pay the clerk, then. You can tell him to expect me."

There was murder in Happy Jack's face, as he glowered at the man who had exposed him publicly as an illiterate. But whatever his impulses, he held them back. A savage swipe of his hand swept the pad and pencil from the bar; he whipped around and without another word strode out of there, leaving the slatted half doors winnowing.

"You rode him pretty hard," Ben Thompson observed as he and Balance started again toward Joe Glennon's office. "The fellow's a yellow rat—but, even a rat will turn if he's cornered."

Balance said, "It was no worse than what you did to him, that day in court—making him pick up Billy's gun and hand it over."

"Maybe." Reminded of the incident, Thompson touched a knuckle to his thick mustache while he pondered it. He finally gave a short laugh, and a shake of his head. "The man is such a bastard, you can't help wanting him to know how much you despise him! Still, as long as he's got the city council behind him, that's a good way to hunt trouble."

"The council," Vern Balance repeated thoughtfully. "When do they meet?"

"Next Tuesday, I guess." Thompson gave him a sharp look. "You got some notion of taking the business of Morco up with those that hired him? For all the good it would do!"

"I didn't say that," Balance answered with a shrug. "Still, it might be interesting." He let the matter rest there.

CHAPTER X

Entering the saloon at eight that night, Balance saw no change from the usual crowd and he caught the bartender's eye to ask, "Anyone in back?" The man gave him a look and a shrug that told him nothing. He went on through the building and beyond the partition, to find that two of the three new card rooms—officially being inaugurated this evening—were dark and empty.

In the third, a poker game was in progress under the yellow glow of the harp lamp—Ben Thompson and Neil Kane and John Sterling, and a couple of Texans that Balance failed to identify. Billy Thompson sat alone in a corner, chair tilted against the wall and a deck of cards in his hand; he looked bored as he pitched them, one by one, into a hat placed on the floor in front of him. The window was open on the summer night, but the air beneath the lamp drifted with layers of cigarette smoke.

From the size of the pot, and the stacks of chips in front of the players, it seemed a desultory game. Balance was not much surprised that Sterling appeared to be the winner—he seldom lost. Ben Thompson, facing the door, gave Balance a brief look over the cards fanned in front of him.

Balance watched the play a moment, found it dull, and turned away to find Joe Glennon standing in the door of his office with a sour expression on his face, and the inevitable cigar building a cloud of smoke about his jowls. As Balance walked over to him, the fat man took the cigar from his mouth long enough to say roughly, "Well, you see how much business we're doing—and on opening night, too! I thought you told me this would bring the big spenders in."

Balance could have pointed out that pouring money into fixing the place up to rival the big-money establishments in Chicago had been no part of his original suggestion; he was feeling let-down, in no mood for holding up his end of a quarrel, and so he merely shrugged and said, "Give it time."

"I just hope we don't go broke while we're waiting!" Glennon retorted and, turning ponderously, disappeared into his office, like a cranky bear waddling into its den, trailing smoke after him.

Vern Balance followed. Glennon had settled into his swivel chair, in front of the account books spread out under the lamp that burned atop the roll-front desk. Going to the window, Balance looked into the early dark and listened to the mutter of sound from the saloon's main room. The mechanical piano was pounding away—Glennon had balked at getting rid of it, but at least had agreed to move the contraption against an outside wall so that the partition, that had served as a sounding board, no longer funneled its racket back here. It was an improvement.

Out of sorts and restless, Balance struck a hand against the sill and turned as Glennon looked up. "If you're staying around anyway," he said, indicating the work spread out in front of his partner, "then there's not too much need for me, here. I'll be back in a couple of hours." He did not wait for an argument; walking out of the office he heard the protesting squeal of the chair pivoting under Glennon's weight, as the fat man swiveled about to watch him go.

He went out through the stale heat and smells of the saloon, looking at no one, and halted a moment under the canopy that roofed the sidewalk. Undecided what he meant to do with himself, he stared across the barren expanse of the plaza where lamplight from the depot's windows made the rails of the switch gleam like molten metal. Over there on North Main, the yawning entry to the livery beckoned.

It decided him. He walked across, and from the hostler on duty ordered the rent buggy hitched up for him.

He started to turn into the west road, that would take him along the river where he had ridden with Tess; but the last thing he wanted just now was to be reminded of her. For the same reason he resolutely avoided looking at the big, three-storied box of lighted windows that was the Drovers Cottage. Instead, he swung to the left on North Main and, as he came abreast of the Grand Central, told himself that if he had any sense he'd move out of the Cottage—bring his stuff over to the other hotel, where he would be spared the constant risk of confronting the girl.

But, if he had any sense he would forget her—though she would be far harder to forget than Lucy Wagoner, the girl in Abilene.

Next door to the Grand Central, a light burned in the tiny building where John Montgomery would be late at work, readying the *Reporter* for press day. Kerosene flares made a fitful wash of light across the façade of the town's barnlike theater; there, bored trailhands would soon be piling in to sit on hard benches, and watch third-rate vaudeville acts from Kansas City.

And then the night closed in as Ellsworth fell behind him, saving only the huddle of cribs and shanties, the dancehall and tawdry saloons that made up Nauchville—the red-light district, just beyond the eastern limits of the town itself.

As he neared, the voice of the place poured at him from open doors and windows, with a note of something near hysteria in it. Vern Balance heard the mix of sound with a hard distaste; he sourly noted the contrast with the calm beauty of the prairie night—moonlit, softened by the glow of stars and outline of trees along the river, cooling earth giving back the clean smells baked into it by the long day's heat.

A regular pattern of hoof tracks, like the spokes of a wheel pointing toward the hub that was Nauchville, showed faintly in the glow of a rising moon. Balance turned north into one of these, and the racket from the raw huddle of buildings fell behind and in a few minutes the night was all about him. He was alone with the slow rhythm of hoofs and turning wheels, the creak of harness and buggy timbers. He let the mare take its own unhurried pace. Insects snapped and buzzed in the brittle weeds; a night bird called, and was still again.

Presently Balance halted the rig and stepped down to the ground. While the mare cropped at grass and weeds, he dug out one of his stogies and got it lit, and walked around looking at the mesh of stars that seemed to press low above his head. Yonder, beyond a slight dip in the prairie, the cookfire of some trail outfit burned with a cherry glow; cattle stirred or lay darkly motionless, and the sound of a harmonica came plaintively on the faint movement of wind across the earth—some cowhand, riding night circle, playing softly to quiet his charges and ease his own boredom.

Moody and at odds with the peacefulness of the night, Vern Balance tramped about as he worked at the cigar. He thought of that cowpuncher, making his music: a young fellow, on his first trip up the trail from Texas; or, perhaps, a grizzled veteran of forty—which was an advanced age at that job. Those who didn't know the life were apt to think of a cowboy as freer and more independent than other men; yet he knew that no one had less to say about his working conditions, or whether he would work at all. The drovers—the stock-owners, the men who spent their time in the plush surroundings of the Drovers Cottage—might gain or lose a hundred thousand dollars on a single herd; the men who had to fight that herd over the trail, and sometimes gave their lives for it in stampede and river crossing, could hope for no more than thirty a month and the chance of being crippled or, at best, worn out and discarded at an age when other men were still considered in their prime.

Yet the drover, too, could be wiped out in a few bad seasons—Balance was reminded of the long faces and the worried talk he heard daily in the lobby of the Drovers Cottage. However you took it, life was a chancy business, and Vern Balance was particularly depressed tonight as he looked at what he had to show for his own: a squandered youth, a killing and a prison term behind him, and his feet directed now in a path that he couldn't see taking him anywhere.

He finished his stogie and angrily stubbed it out against a buggy tire, before tossing it aside into the weeds. He was doing himself no good, brooding here alone; and he did have an obligation of sorts toward Joe Glennon, and the partnership he hadn't actually wanted. Balance shrugged and climbed again into the buggy, and turned the mare back toward town.

Within sight of the lights of Nauchville, the hubbub of the place swelling toward him across the short remaining distance, he all at once pulled in so sharply that the mare tossed its head in protest. With the buggy's noise stilled he could hear more plainly, now, a sound of running footsteps. He ducked his head and leaned forward, trying to line up the lights of the dancehall less than a quarter mile away; as he did so, behind the footsteps the rhythmic drumming of a horse's hoofs began to swell, coming at a steady lope, and growing quickly louder.

Suddenly he could see the runner already so close that he caught the sound of sobbing, panting breath. There was a glimpse only, but enough to convince him it was a woman; next moment the horse had overtaken her, a bulky shape against the moon's shadows, and when she tried to duck aside the rider swerved—deliberately, Balance thought. The shoulder of the animal struck her and, with a cry of terror, she was hurled off her feet.

The rider left saddle and impetus carried the horse on, so that it narrowly missed colliding headfirst with the buggy mare; and Balance had to give attention to his own animal. Then he had it settled, and he could hear the sounds of a nearby struggle—a man's voice exploding in anger, the strike of a blow.

The sensible thing would have been to stay out of it, but a whimpering gasp of pain from the woman stirred a male instinct in him and brought him down from the buggy, not forgetting to palm the short-barreled Colt from his shoulder harness as he strode forward. "What's going on here?" he demanded loudly, and suddenly everything stopped.

There were no trees, and little brush—hardly anything to break the sweep of night wind through the brittle, sun-cooked grass, or to dilute the spread of moonlight. Now that he was out from under the buggy's top, he could see both the man and the woman clearly enough. They broke apart, the man releasing his grasp and turning to meet him.

Balance thought he could guess all he needed to know about the woman from the way she was dressed—her throat and shoulders gleaming like pale ivory—and from the aroma of cheap perfume. Her cheeks had dark blotches that would probably be rouge; but something even darker was spilling a track from a corner of her mouth, and that filled him with anger toward any man who would be the cause of such a thing.

Especially a man as big as this one. At first Balance had an impression of broad, high shoulders, of the head set solidly atop a deep and massive chest. It was only then that something about the silhouette struck him as familiar; while Ernie Telford, for his part, seemed to recognize the smaller man at once. A grunt of surprise broke from him, and Clayt Spearman's trail boss threw back his head so that the shadow of his hatbrim slid away and revealed his face— the curiously flat features, the bulging eyes wide-set above high cheekbones, the jaw that widened at the hinges.

"Well, I'll be damned!" he muttered. "It *is* you!"

"Yes, it's me, Telford."

"I ain't surprised. I get back from Wichita and hardly catch my breath, before people start letting me know you're out of the pen and bent on making more trouble . . ."

Balance chose to ignore that. He asked, "Is Clayt with you?"

"He will be. He's in K.C., at the moment. Well, there's going to be *one* piece of news that'll interest him—that is, if you've got nerve enough to be around when he gets here."

"I wasn't thinking of going anywhere," Balance answered bluntly. "Not right away, that I know of." He turned to the woman, then. "Are you all right?"

She was staring at him, speechless. Blustering, Ernie Telford said loudly, "Just stay out of things that are none of your goddam business!"

"I'd be less than a man," he snapped, "not to interfere when I see a woman being roughed up. How bad did he hurt you?" he demanded, looking at her again.

This time she found her voice. "It ain't anything."

"From the sound it made when he hit you, he might almost have broken your jaw. And, your lip is bleeding." She touched the back of her hand to it; perhaps she was only drunk, but to Vern Balance she seemed, rather, in a daze. Knowing the violent temper of Clayt Spearman's trail boss, he was suddenly reluctant to leave them together. "It's your affair," he told her, "but I think you better come with me. I'll see that you get home. What about it?"

She hesitated. "I'll go with you."

Telford swore at that, and actually raised an arm as though to hit her again. Balance lifted the gun a little and its barrel glinted. The big man's head swiveled to look at it. He said heavily, "I got no gun with me."

"Well, I have," Balance said. "But not much patience—nor much stomach for walking away and letting a woman get beat up."

"Put that thing away," Telford suggested, "and I'll break you in two! Would you like that better?"

"I'm not looking for trouble with you, but I won't back away from it either. Nor will I put up the gun. Why don't you just go see what became of your horse, and forget this business?"

"Cheap, murderin', tinhorn bastard!" Ernie Telford's voice was roughened by the liquor that he had been drinking, and that hung about him in a fog. "There's plenty you damn' well ain't going to be allowed to forget! I promise you!" But Balance's reminder about his horse must have broken through to him. The trail boss swore again, and swung his heavy shoulders and went tramping past in the direction where his animal had disappeared.

Vern Balance made a half turn to watch him go, the gun swiveling to follow him. Afterward, he slid the gun back into its holster as he looked again at the woman.

She could scarcely have been cold, yet he saw her rubbing the flesh of her bare upper arms and he thought she was shivering. Her voice held a tremor of near hysteria. "I'm really scared of Ernie when he's like that!"

"Well, we're rid of him now." But as he said it he knew how hollow that was. The woman was plainly nothing but a Nauchville prostitute, and any time Ernie Telford wanted to get his hands on her there was really nothing she could do about it. "My rig's over this way," he added gruffly.

She took a step, caught herself with a gasp of pain; she would have gone down, the pointed heel of her slipper turning on the uneven ground, if Balance hadn't caught her arm. "I guess I twisted my ankle when I fell," she said on a ragged intake of breath. "I'll be all right . . ."

But he kept hold of her, supporting her weight, until they had reached the buggy and he helped her onto the seat. He went around and climbed in beside her. Taking out his handkerchief he said, "Use this on that lip, if it's still bleeding."

She accepted it, with a murmured thanks; and as he picked up the reins she added, in a voice muffled against the folds of the handker-chief, "I'll tell you where to drop me."

"All right."

He clucked to the mare and they rolled ahead, toward the lights of the buildings. Vern Balance found himself wondering about Ernie Telford. He must have caught up his horse, by this time; so, where was he? Going to look for a gun? he thought, and didn't like the implications.

But he said nothing and after a moment the woman spoke, hesi-tantly. "Mister, I'm sorry if I got you into trouble with Ernie Tel-ford!"

He shrugged. "Nothing was apt to get me in any worse than I al-ready am, with him or with the outfit he works for."

She said, unexpectedly, "You shot that Bud Spearman youngster, didn't you—in Abilene?" He could feel her looking at him. When he nodded she said, "I thought so. Ernie told me something about it." She didn't elaborate.

"Did he cut your lip bad?" Balance asked, after a moment, and saw her shake her head though she still held the handkerchief against it. "I always took him for a tough man, especially when he'd been drinking too much; I suppose it needs someone like that, to push a herd and a crew of hardcase Texans all that distance. But I don't understand a man who'd take his meanness out the way I saw him do tonight!"

"Person like me gets used to that," she said, a tired edge coming into her voice. "As for Ernie, he probably thought I had it coming. But, I ain't his personal property—I don't care *what* he thinks! None of his business what I do when he ain't around!"

So that was it, Balance thought with a twinge of distaste. It was about what he had supposed: jealousy over a Nauchville prostitute —suspicion about her behavior, during the time he was in Wichita— driving a violent man past control of his temper. He wanted to know nothing more about the matter, and he asked no further questions.

Perhaps she sensed this, for as they came to the first of the huddle of buildings she said briefly, "You can let me out anywhere."

"Not with that ankle," Balance told her. "You shouldn't be walk-ing on it. I'll put you down at your door."

He felt the scrutiny she gave him. "All right," she said, in an odd tone, and gave the directions.

They turned into a rutted alley and pulled up at the entrance of a drab frame box of a building. There were lights showing, upstairs and down, and through the open windows of the parlor came the reedy sounds of a badly played concertina, and too-loud voices—male and female. The woman moved to climb out of the buggy but Vern Balance knew she would not be able to make it without help. He got down and came around and gave her a hand, afterward keeping hold of her arm to steady her on the warped and uneven boards of the sidewalk.

Light from a window showed her more clearly. He thought she was older than he, though life could have aged her. She might almost have been pretty, once; the bruised swelling that was beginning now to throw the left side of her face out of shape was no help. She showed him the handkerchief he had given her, wadded in one hand and marked with blood. "I'll wash this and return it."

"No need to bother," he told her gruffly.

Her eyes on his face, she said, "It's been a long time since anyone treated me as much like a lady, as you done tonight!"

He was touched by her gratitude, but it embarrassed him too; he was afraid she might offer to repay him in a manner that he would have to refuse, and he didn't want to hurt her any more than she already had been. He asked, "What's your name?"

"Angie . . ."

"Well, Angie, I'm sorry about tonight. I'm only glad I was able to step in before Ernie Telford had time to do anything worse."

"I wouldn't want you havin' more trouble," she said, "account of me."

"Don't worry about it," he told her. "Any trouble I may have with Clayt Spearman's outfit, there's no cause to blame yourself." He added bruskly, "If you're OK now, it's time I was going. I have to get back to work."

She nodded. When he stepped back into the buggy, and got the mare into motion, the woman was still standing in front of the door with his handkerchief clutched in her fist. He saw her there as he turned the corner, and put her from his sight.

It had proved to be a quiet and uneventful evening at the Oriental Palace, with no more than the usual number of customers and the usual drunken fight or two, that had to be broken up before they could get out of hand. The poker game in Ben Thompson's card room lasted until shortly after midnight, leading to nothing of any particular interest; then it closed down and all three of the new rooms were dark and silent.

Vern Balance had kept an uneasy watch for Ernie Telford, expecting at any moment to see him come looking for Bud Spearman's killer —with a gun, this time, and perhaps with the Rafter 7 crew at his back. But there had been no sign of him. At one o'clock, with business virtually over for the night, Balance walked the short block to his room at the Drovers Cottage and the street lay almost silent in the stillness of the August night.

But as he lay naked and sweating on sheets that were almost too hot to touch, with the breathless weight of heat pressing down upon him from the low ceiling and scarcely a hint of breeze stirring the curtains, a board creaked outside his door and a hand turned the knob, cautiously. At once he rolled over, bed springs squealing, and the gun that had been hanging in its harness on the nearby chairback slid into his hand. On his belly now, elbows bent, he propped the gun in front of him and thumbed the hammer back and said—just loudly enough that he knew his voice would carry beyond the closed panel, "All right, there's a gun pointed at the door. Come on in, if you think you have to!"

He waited. No sound, for long moments; he could hear his own breathing, and feel the thud of his heartbeat against the mattress. Then the hand that held the knob let its spring turn it slowly back, and released it. There was the muffled sound of footsteps prowling away down the hall, quickly silenced.

By the time Balance could reach the door and get it unlocked and opened a crack, the hallway lay empty in the dim glow from a couple of turned-down oil lamps in wall holders. Had it been an enemy? Or someone too whiskey-fuddled to know his own room, and too terrified at Balance's warning to do anything but retreat? There was no way to tell; he closed the door again and turned the key, and then padded barefoot to the window for a look past the gallery roof, into the plaza. Nothing to be seen there, either.

He rubbed his cheek thoughtfully with the muzzle of the gun, and then shrugged and turned away. Whoever it was, he was fairly sure he had given them a start; he had shown that the occupant of this room was less than a sound sleeper. His caller would have to think about that. Nevertheless, when he lay down again the chair was propped beneath the knob of the door, and the gun was under his pillow.

CHAPTER XI

On Tuesday it actually seemed for a while that the heat might break. In late afternoon, clouds had gathered—a tumbled pile of thunderheads, sooty black at their base and as pure white as whipped cream where they towered against the deep dome of the sky. When Vern Balance walked across the plaza, to the meeting in the council room above the drygoods store, he could see lightning pulsate within the pearly depths of the cloud mass. He had hoped, with the rest of Ellsworth, that a rain would come out of it that would drench the dry prairie and the sun-scorched buildings of the village.

Instead, a mere handful of drops had shaken down to make dark splotches in the dust, the size of silver dollars; then the clouds sailed majestically on, driven by a turmoil of winds that never touched the earth. They left in their wake a heightened tension and an oppressive humidity, that was worse than what had been before.

This matched Balance's mood as he stood now at the window of Glennon's office, scowling into the night and thinking about that council meeting. Likely it had been a mistake to go; at least he supposed he should have kept his mouth shut. But sight of the five men gathered around the table, listlessly discussing how best to clear trash off the town's vacant lots, had triggered a reaction and brought him forward to make an angry complaint against Happy Jack Morco.

The mayor, a man named James Miller who bore the look of a small-town real estate promoter, had tried to call him out of order, but he insisted on being heard. "My partner and I run a respectable place of business; we can keep order there without interference from some illiterate bully with a badge pinned on him. This afternoon he tried to bull his way into the Oriental Palace—and he was so drunk I wouldn't let him in."

His friend Jim Gore was nodding approval, but he got only scowls from the other councilmen. A druggist named Ward Linker said loudly, "Morco has full authority to enter any business house south of the K.P. tracks. That's his beat."

"Then give him another one," Balance retorted, his temper flaring. "Let him mop out the jail . . . only, keep him away from the Palace! In fact, if you take my advice, you won't let him set foot south of those tracks—or someday you may be sorry."

"Are you threatening this council?" snapped Linker.

"Of course not. I'm just saying that Morco is deliberately making enemies of the Texans. And that's certainly no way to keep the peace!"

The whole table fell into an uproar—a one-sided squabble, with Jim Gore the only councilman supporting Balance's argument. He understood now what Gore had told him about politics in this town. The mayor was slamming the table with an inkwell, trying to bring some kind of order to the meeting, when Balance disgustedly turned his back and walked out.

Dusk was settling by then, lamplight beginning to spot the shadows; and Balance had felt a certain amount of uneasiness as he walked back across the darkening plaza toward the Oriental Palace.

He had left his gun on Glennon's desk, feeling it would be a poor business to wear a weapon into council meeting in deliberate defiance of the council's own ordinance; but he missed the now-familiar weight and bulk of it under his arm, and it left him vulnerable as long as he did not know just what to expect from Ernie Telford. He found it hard to keep from looking over his shoulder, and starting at noises.

Telford, he firmly believed, was the one who had tried to enter his hotel room after their confrontation over the Nauchville woman. In the days since then he had seen the big fellow a number of times —going in and out of the saloons, or riding through the plaza with Chick Potter or others of his particular friends in the Rafter 7 crew. Telford had never so much as given a sign of recognition, and to Vern Balance that could only mean that he was playing some deep game of his own. The trail boss was not one to forget a grievance. He might be letting Balance stew and wait for his move; on the other hand, he might simply be marking time until Clayt Spearman returned. Spearman, after all, was Telford's boss, and would claim first right to the killer of his son. The more Balance thought about it, the more he was inclined to think this must be the reason Ernie Telford was holding off.

Standing now at the window in Glennon's office, Balance said softly, "Damn!"

When he stepped off the train in July, with two years of prison behind him, he had thought himself a free man again; yet here he was, up to his neck in a troubled complex of affairs. He scowled as he took one of his stogies from his pocket. The normal sounds of the barroom came to him, and a burst of talk from Ben Thompson's games across the hall, where all three card rooms were busy this evening. Balance canted his head to listen.

At least, that investment was finally beginning to pay off. More and more of the Texas drovers, made reckless by weeks of futile waiting, were spending long hours at Ben's tables playing for high stakes with money they'd borrowed from the Ellsworth banks at usurious rates. A percentage of every pot raked in, regardless of who won or lost, went into the profits of the house to become a dividend on Vern Balance's investment; yet, somehow, it didn't give him much real satisfaction.

After all, these were desperate men, facing disaster. It was sad to think of them drinking too much, betting too steeply, trying to down their tensions; he wondered how soon they would run out of cash and start betting their herds—so many head for a white chip, and no man knowing whether the cattle he wagered was worth a fortune, or perhaps nothing at all . . .

Biting off the end of the cigar he told himself that, for a man who only wanted freedom and his life kept simple, he was certainly managing to get himself entangled—not only in his own problems, but other people's as well!

Restless and sweating and irritable, Balance fired up his smoke and walked out into the barroom, to gauge the mood of the place— the trailhands drinking here tonight seemed just as bad tempered as their worried bosses in the card rooms. He had paused to get his stogie to drawing better, and was moving to the bar for a word with the houseman on duty, when a disturbance broke out by the main door. Instantly he changed directions without breaking stride, hand slipping automatically toward his gun—he had made his boast to the council about keeping order at the Palace without any help from the city's police, and he was determined to make good on it.

It would have been hard to say what had started the trouble this time; two sworn enemies, perhaps, colliding by accident in the doorway and at once tearing into each other while a leaf of the green-painted half doors slammed back against the wall. Balance reached them, said "All right—that's enough!" and, seizing one of the brawlers, bulled him through the opening and onto the sidewalk outside. The gun was in his hand; the swing door flapped shut behind them as he told the puncher, "You want to fight, there are plenty of other places along the street. It doesn't go here!"

And then, aware of a presence at his back, he started to turn but it was already too late. Breath sucked in through his jaws as he felt the hard ring of a gun's muzzle against his spine. The voice at his ear gave a hoarse order: "Drop the gun, or this one will blow a hole right through you!"

He didn't try to look around; he understood what had happened to him, easily enough. The staging of the fight in the doorway had been cued to his appearance in the main room; they had known he would have to move to stop it, and they couldn't have planned it any simpler to maneuver him outside where they wanted him. He dropped his hand from the first man's shoulder, and at the same moment felt the gun snatched from his fingers by the other who had crowded out close behind him.

He said gruffly, "All right, you worked that well! Now, what do you two think you want from me?"

Just a moment ago they had been tearing at each other like deadly enemies. Now one laughed shortly and said, "We'll show you. Start walking." He was given a shove in the direction they wanted.

Balance, giving with it, seemed to trip on the warped planks of the walk. He fell aside and his elbow sank into the middle of the one who held the guns. The man grunted and dropped back a step; Balance thought for an instant he would break into the clear. Then a fist sledged him where his neck joined the shoulder, and he stumbled and went down.

He tried to roll free but the legs of one of his captors stopped him. Hands seized and hauled him up. He felt almost as though his shoulder had been dislocated; still he fought, desperately, with elbows and fists, but they allowed him only a second or two of that before a gun's barrel struck him across the ear. Pain rang through his head, like a bell. All the fight leaked out of him and then he was being half carried, feet dragging, over the rattling sidewalk timbers and quickly into the darkness of the alleyway adjoining the Palace.

Despite his resistance, the capture could have taken no more than half a minute. One of the men, speaking above his head, muttered gustily, "You reckon anybody saw that?"

"Ain't likely," the other answered. Balance felt himself shaken and set on his feet, and when his legs started to go the flat of a hand struck his face, one side and then the other. The first voice told him harshly, "You better start walking if you know what's good for you. We sure as hell ain't carrying you!"

It was a Texas voice; and now he thought he recognized it. He thought it sounded very much like Ernie Telford's friend, Chick Potter.

The fog inside his skull had dissipated under the stinging of the slaps; his vision cleared and he found his legs could support him, at least after a fashion. Potter grunted, "That's a little better. Now—come along." And with a hand clamped on either arm they marched him off, steadying him as they hurried him over the dark and uneven ground.

In the beginning, Balance understood, Ellsworth had been constructed at a natural ford where the military road crossed the Smoky Hill; but in the first year the river had flooded and swept the town away and it had to be rebuilt, a safe distance back from the steeply eroded bank. Now, as they passed a few sheds and outhouses, the town raveled out and there was nothing and no one to hinder his captors. He could smell the mud of the shrunken river and hear frogs croaking in the shallows, before the dark line of cottonwoods showed dimly.

There was no moon tonight—only an occasional fitful gleam of lightning flickering along the low horizon beyond the river and the trees. But his captors knew where they were going. They swung west and presently, through the shifting trunks, Balance saw a point of light. Moments later he made out a small clot of men and horses waiting above the dropoff of the bank. The light resolved itself into a buggy lamp, fastened to the frame of a blacktopped rig; a horse stood patiently between the shafts, head bent to nibble at the rank grass.

Now he was close enough to recognize the horse and buggy—ironically enough, it was the same outfit he himself had rented from the livery on a couple of occasions. A man's face, just touched by the lanternglow, looked at him from the shadowy interior. He did not have to be told whose it was.

He was marched up to the buggy and brought to a stand there. Chick Potter said, "We brung him, Clayt. Sorry if we kept you waiting."

"I've waited two years," the man on the buggy's seat answered briefly. "A few minutes more don't matter!"

He sat forward now, moving into the light. The lantern showed Clayt Spearman's blocky, handsome features—reminiscent of both his daughter and his dead son: the well-carved brow and solid jaw, the thick mustache and luxuriant mop of hair that had turned a rich, ivory white. His hands, callused and rope-scarred, gripped the handle of the cane that stood upright between his damaged knees and he leaned above it, keen brown eyes pinned on the face of the man his trailhands had delivered to him.

Vern Balance said coldly, "I don't have to ask what this is all about!"

The stare raked him, with a kind of gloating intensity. He could imagine what he looked like at the moment. His head still rang from the blow with the gunbarrel; his ear and cheek felt as though they must be swollen several times beyond their natural size, and there was a warm wetness of blood where the weapon's front sight had torn the skin. Clayt Spearman told him, in a voice that held all his fierce satisfaction: "Mister, I vowed that day in the Abilene courtroom that I'd have my chance at you—*some*time, however long it might be in coming!"

In the silence, the croaking of frogs seemed very loud, and the stirring of branches overhead, and the stamp and rustle of horses foraging as they waited. The men, also, waited. Spearman must have brought every hand he could spare from the trail camp, Balance decided—he had wanted them to see this. Now one stepped out of the background, and the glow of the buggy lamp picked him up; it revealed the big shape and the broad face of Ernie Telford, and also the coil of hemp rope swinging in his hands.

"So it's a lynching," Vern Balance said.

Telford's teeth showed, faintly white, behind his grin. "No," he corrected. "An execution." With a backhand gesture he slapped the rope coil against the trunk of a huge cottonwood that rose toward the dark sky. "In case you hadn't heard, this here was Ellsworth's official hangin' tree, in the early days. That's why we had you brung here, mister. Seems fitting—you won't be the first murderer to get strung up from it."

His hands played lovingly with the rope, shaking out the coils, and Balance felt his mouth go dry. And now Telford stepped back from the tree, peering up. One stout branch thrust out from the trunk at a convenient height, showing all too clearly why that tree had been chosen for its particular purpose. With a rope handler's expert cast, Telford flipped the coil up and over; it whispered in summer-dry leaves and then dropped where he wanted it, the loop swinging gently.

"Nobody owes you a damn' thing," Clayt Spearman told the prisoner harshly. "You stand convicted of the killing of my son—only, justice has a way of being slow about getting carried out sometimes. Still, if you got anything you want to say first, I suppose we'll listen."

Balance tore his eyes away from the noose. A cold trickling of sweat had broken out beneath his shirt, but he managed to keep his voice level as he looked at the old man on the buggy's seat and said bluntly, "I already told you, that day in court, I was sorry for what happened to Bud Spearman—and that I never meant to kill him. I'll say it again now. But, I won't beg!"

Chick Potter suggested with cruel humor, "Maybe he'll beg a little when he actually feels the rope!"

The old man, studying the prisoner with those fierce, hating eyes, shook his head. "No," he decided, "somehow I doubt that." He shifted his position on the leather seat then, and told Ernie Telford impatiently, "Get on with it!"

Suddenly, the preliminaries and the talk were over. Hands seized Balance and dragged him to the tree, in a quick, fierce struggle of scuffing boots and panting breaths. Silently he fought them, flattened one man with a wild swing of an arm that he managed to free. But they were too many, and too imbued with Spearman's implacable purpose. Someone gritted, "Damn it, *hold him!*" A fist struck him in the face, cutting his lip on a tooth and filling his mouth with the hot taste of his own blood. And then the rope hung before his eyes, and he was trying to twist his head away from it as hands spread the noose and forced it down into place.

Then everything stopped.

Breathing hard, Balance raised his head and peered through sweat and streaming hair at the man who had walked into the circle of light from the buggy lamp. For that frozen moment, no one spoke or moved though the hands continued to hold him fast. And then Sheriff Whitney said, in a shocked voice, "For the love of God, what do you men think you're doing?"

"What does it look like we're doing?" Clayt Spearman retorted. He added, "No one asked you to interfere!"

"Do you expect me not to?" the sheriff said. "You're outside the town limits, which puts this in the county—in my jurisdiction. And I'm telling you to take your hands off that man!"

"Why, hell, Sheriff!" Ernie Telford said, the rope's end ready in his fists; his voice held a boisterous aggressiveness but to Balance it sounded suddenly ill at ease. "We're just borrowing your tree for the purpose it was always used for."

"Never in *my* time," the lawman replied. "And not now!" He came resolutely ahead—a slight, bearded figure, obviously unarmed and alone against the anger of the Texans; yet no one seemed ready actively to oppose him. He came and placed a hand on the rope, and when Telford refused to relinquish it he looked over at the crippled rancher in the buggy.

Clayt Spearman swore at him, an outcry that was all but choked with rage. But the protest died, and when he fell silent Cap Whitney, quite deliberately, took the noose from around the prisoner's neck and left the rope useless in Telford's hands. He brushed aside Chick

Potter's hold, and Vern Balance stepped free on legs that were suddenly far from steady.

Balance spat out a mouthful of blood, and put a hand to his throat. Looking from the sheriff to the old man in the buggy, he knew that whatever happened now would be, somehow, between those two.

He thought Clayt Spearman would climb out of the buggy, crippled legs or not. Clayt lifted his stick in a hand that shook. "Taking my rope off his neck don't mean the end of this, Whitney!" he shouted. "You won't always be around to save his hide for him!"

"He knows that," the sheriff answered calmly. "But after this he also knows what to expect from you."

"I won't be quite as easy to take, a second time!" Vern Balance promised grimly. He looked at Chick Potter. "You've got something of mine," he said coldly, and held out his hand for it.

The puncher glowered, shot a glance at his boss and at Ernie Telford but got no signals from either. With a shrug, he pulled the short-barreled Colt he had tucked behind his belt and handed it over; and then he backed away a step, as though he guessed Balance's wild impulse to hit and even the score for the swollen ear, and the pain that still throbbed in his head.

But Balance was past crude revenge, and he turned away to tell the sheriff, "I don't know what caused you to show when you did, but it was a lucky thing for me."

The bearded man shook his head. "You made your own luck, by putting up a fight there in front of the Palace. That's what caught my attention—but when I tried to follow where they'd taken you, I got lost until I remembered this tree." He looked up at the branch, and the noose still swaying from it. He said, "I think maybe it's time that damned thing was cut down!"

"There's other trees," Ernie Telford muttered.

But no one looked at him. Their purposes thwarted by the sheriff's arrival, the fight seemed for the moment to have gone out of them. Only Clayt Spearman still had something to say; he pointed his stick at Balance and spoke in a voice freighted with warning: "One last word for you, mister! I know about you and my daughter— I heard you been seen with her, taking advantage of the fact she wasn't aware who you really were. Well, she's been told—I seen to that! And I don't want to hear of you bothering her again. You understand me?"

Vern Balance thought: So now she knows! In a way it was almost a relief to have the matter settled, and though he would always wonder how she had taken it there was little likelihood of his ever finding out. Now he merely shrugged and told Clayt Spearman bluntly, "No need to worry that I'd hurt your daughter. I only wish I'd never laid eyes on any of your family!"

Turning from the hostile stares of the old man and his crew, he caught the sheriff's troubled frown and put his thanks into a nod. After that he tramped away, alone, in the direction of Ellsworth's scattered lights.

CHAPTER XII

He was standing before the mirror in his room, using his razor and charily mindful of the still-swollen, still-aching juncture of jaw hinge and cheekbone, when the popping of a handgun in the quiet took him to the window for a look down into the plaza.

The dusty stretch in front of the Drovers Cottage was deserted and still, except for a single, bareheaded figure moving about in early morning sunshine—a trailhand, obviously still feeling the effects of the cheap busthead liquor someone had been selling him the night before; he looked small and ineffectual and lonely down there, with his unbuttoned shirt half off him and a gun hanging in his fist. He was talking to himself, singing an occasional snatch of incoherent song as he wandered in aimless circles, jerking into motion and halting again.

He saw an empty can lying in the dust, winking back the sunlight; he tried to set it rolling with a shot that missed and kicked dirt a good yard wide of the mark. He walked up to the can, shooting and missing again, and finally gave the thing a kick with his boot. And as he lifted his head and stood weaving, blearily hunting more targets, another man moved into Balance's range. Unseen as yet by the drunken Texan, this one was coming at him from the north side of the plaza, with definite purpose. It was Happy Jack Morco, the high sun bouncing a smear of glitter from the badge fastened to his vest.

Vern Balance knew what was coming. Eyes narrowed, he coldly watched the drama unfolding below him.

The cowboy had settled on the sign fronting Jake New's saloon, and was trying to draw a bead on it, sighting down the full length of an arm that seemed too unsteady for his eye to locate the gun at its end. He was concentrating on this when Morco walked up behind him; Morco's hand descended on the man's shoulder and hauled him around, so abruptly that he tangled his boots and staggered to keep from falling. The arm dropped to his side as he stood unsteadily facing the deputy; an argument began.

From this window, Balance could hear only an angry word or two from Happy Jack, the mumble of the drunk's incoherent answers. Over a drawn six-shooter, Morco was apparently ordering the cowboy to surrender his weapon; the latter was shaking his head, protesting. And at last he simply turned his back and started to walk away.

Instantly Morco pounced.

Vern Balance was sure he meant to club the man from behind with his gunbarrel. Instead, Happy Jack caught the cowboy's arm and wrenched it high between his shoulders; there was a thin squawl of pain and the man's knees started to buckle. And then, having holstered his own revolver, Morco deftly snatched his victim's weapon from his fingers and rammed him forcibly in the back with it. Without ceremony, the Texan was spun around and marched off across the plaza at a stumbling, bent-over trot—his arm still pinioned, heading for jail and another two-dollar fine for the deputy's pocket.

If there had been any question, Vern Balance knew now just how much effect he and Jim Gore had had with the city council: none at all, so far as Happy Jack Morco was concerned.

He turned from the window, with an angry grimace and a shrug for the question of Ellsworth's police force. He had enough problems of his own to concern him. He finished with the razor and toweled the soap from his face, satisfied at least that the swelling that made his cheek appear faintly lopsided had subsided, though the hinge popped occasionally when he worked his jaw. He supposed he could be thankful that he had taken no worse damage.

Afterward, in the corridor, he stopped to stare a moment at the door he thought of as Tess Spearman's. He wondered what he would say or do, were she suddenly to open it and confront him. He could hear no sound from in there; maybe her father had already taken her out of the Drovers Cottage, furious with the Gores for letting her have anything to do with the killer of his son. Not for the first time, he thought perhaps he ought to move out himself—go across the plaza to the Grand Central. Yet, there was a stubborn streak in Vern Balance, that insisted he was minding his own business and had as much right to be where he was, as anyone else.

Still he found himself tensed as he went down the stairs into the lobby. There was no sign of the Spearmans there, or in the dining room. He took a corner table, and ordered a breakfast of eggs and sausage. He was nearly finished with it when Joe Glennon came in.

Glennon looked anxious. He peered around, located Balance's table and quickly made his way over there; sliding into the empty chair he dropped his hands upon the tablecloth and stared across the table at his partner. "Bad news?" the latter suggested dryly.

"For you," Glennon said. He shook his head at the waitress who came to see if he wanted to order, and frowned as Balance speared a last piece of sausage and reached for coffee to wash it down. "What did you do to Clayt Spearman, last night?"

"It's more a question of what he nearly did to me! At any rate, it's over and done with."

"You think so?" the other retorted. "From what I hear, more likely it's just started! Would you believe Clayt Spearman's gone and put a bounty on you?"

Balance slowly put down the cup. "Where did you hear a thing like that?"

"From more than one source, I can tell you—I've been hearing nothing else, all morning. The man that downs you is supposed to get five hundred cash. Spearman's past wanting you brought to him alive. He wants you *dead!*"

Vern Balance told himself the slow crawling he felt in his gut was not actually the beginning of fear, but more a kind of horror at the full realization of Spearman's hatred. Of course, the report might not be true—it was the kind of rumor that was almost certain to start, in the wake of last night's events. Everything in him rebelled against believing it.

Joe Glennon, for one, surely believed it. He was breathing with effort, his fingers drumming the tablecloth. "So I figured you should know about this," he was saying. "Assuming you didn't already . . ."

"And you took it on yourself?" It would have cost the fat man a real physical effort to go prowling about the town, carrying messages in the sultry August morning's heat. Balance was suddenly quite touched, remembering that he had once accused this man of actually plotting his death.

"It seemed only decent," Glennon answered gruffly.

"Thanks." He used his napkin, put money on the table, pushed back his chair. "I appreciate it, whether there's really anything in this or not."

"Then you *don't* believe it!" Joe Glennon sounded irritable as he followed his partner into the lobby.

"If a man doesn't look out, he can get so he believes almost anything of anyone," Balance said. "But I promise I'll keep my eyes open."

"Don't do it for me! It's *your* neck—but at least, I told you . . ."

Vern Balance was all too well aware of the stares that followed them as they left the hotel, to walk the short block to the Palace. They passed men who broke off conversations to watch them silently by. It did seem that, true or not, a lot of people had heard the rumors of Clayt Spearman's bounty offer.

And then, turning in at the Palace, he pushed open the slotted doors and knew at once that the rumors were true, and that he should have heeded them.

Chick Potter, and another man whom he remembered from the scene beneath the hanging tree, stood at the bar with filled glasses by their elbows. They had an air of waiting for something rather than being there to enjoy themselves; what the something might be, was quickly plain from the way they both turned to face the door. And now a third man rose from his seat at the nearest table—the deliberate and unhurried way in which he moved, he seemed almost to grow toward the ceiling: Few men bulked much bigger than Ernie Telford.

All three were armed.

Retreat at this point would have been difficult. Balance halted, just inside the door, and in a sweeping glance saw that the room was otherwise all but deserted—there was the bartender, polishing glasses behind the counter, and at a table against the farther wall, Ben Thompson's friends Neil Kane and Cad Pierce seated with a bottle between them. They seemed to take only an idle interest in what was building here.

Ernie Telford said, "We was beginning to wonder if you figured to come in, this morning. Thought we might have to go over to the Cottage and get you."

"I think you tried that once before," Vern Balance said.

If Telford knew he was referring to the night when a hand tested the knob of his door and then withdrew at his challenge, the big man gave no sign. Balance risked a glance toward Joe Glennon, who had come in behind him. His partner had drawn quickly aside and was standing clear, his cheeks faintly shining with sweat, his hands spread in plain view: He was showing that he took no part in this. Monty, the bartender, had dropped his towel and placed both palms flat on the counter. Vern Balance was alone.

He said dryly, "That five hundred won't amount to much, split so many ways."

"I imagine the old man can be got to raise it," Ernie Telford said. He turned and stared for a long moment at the two Texans seated at that other table, as though trying to judge what to expect from them.

For his part, Balance had no question. Pierce and Kane were Ben Thompson's friends, not his. The trouble he might have got himself into was nothing to them.

Now Chick Potter put in a warning: "Watch his hands, Ernie. There's a gun under that coat."

Telford pulled his attention again to the prisoner. "I know about the gun," he said; and to the third rider, who was closest: "Lewt, how about you ease over there and get it."

Someone said, "How about you stay where you are . . ."

Ernie Telford stiffened, his head jerking as though someone had rammed a fist into his spine. None of the three Spearman riders seemed to have heard that door at the back of the room as it opened, or the newcomer's quiet entrance. Slowly, now, the trail boss made a quarter turn and froze as he saw Ben Thompson, and the double-snouted English shotgun pointed at his head. At the sight his broad cheeks slowly drained of color.

Still, Ernie Telford did not break that easily. His scowl deepened and he demanded, "What business would this be of yours?"

"Why, it's just that," Thompson said. "Business! Long as I run the games here, I have a natural interest in the man who's half owner of the establishment. So, I think you fellows had better get off of him."

Scowling and hesitant, Telford let the fingers of his right hand run nervously across the ball of the thumb, just above the outthrust handle of his holstered gun. "Hell, Ben!" he protested, almost plaintively. "You and me are *Texans!* And so was the boy this Yankee bastard murdered. Don't that mean nothing?"

Thompson answered without any change of tone or expression: "I never gave much of a damn for Bud Spearman, wherever he was from. And Vern Balance is by way of being a friend of mine." He indicated Telford's companions. "Why don't you take these two pistols, and the lot of you just get out of here and forget to come back!"

For a moment, no one moved. A pinched, wild look had come into Ernie Telford's eyes. And now, chair legs scraped loudly and Cad Pierce and Neil Kane eased to their feet. A wink of blued steel appeared in the latter's hand; he said quietly, "Telford, you're boxed!"

The big trail boss jerked about to stare at him. Cad Pierce's gun was still in the holster but Pierce had his fingers wrapped around the handle. Ernie Telford seemed to get the message. His heavy shoulders settled. "So that's how it is!" he grunted. A deep breath swelled his chest and he looked murderously at Balance—an angry man, cheated of his victim. "It pays to have tough friends."

"*You* didn't exactly come alone," Vern Balance reminded him.

Ben Thompson said crisply, "And if you come again, you'd better bring more! As I told you, this interferes with business—so either you leave Balance alone, or count me in, too!"

The big man studied him a moment, testing the gambler's purpose. Their stares held, locked; then Ernie Telford muttered an obscenity and, swinging his powerful shoulders, motioned to his men. Balance stepped aside. The three filed past him, without a backward glance, and tramped out leaving the panels winnowing.

There was the sound of a released breath that fluttered Joe Glennon's cheeks. For his part, Vern Balance was very close to anger as he turned to Ben Thompson. "Look!" he exclaimed. "I don't mean to have you—or anyone—stand between me and my enemies!"

Thompson merely shrugged and he let the hammers of the shotgun off cock. It was Glennon who told Balance, "Don't be a fool! It's the cheapest insurance you could buy. Nobody's going to make a move against you, if they know it would mean a runin with Ben Thompson."

"A man expects to face his own problems."

"A man can wind up dead, too . . ."

Balance gave his partner a cold look, afterward walking back to the table where Ben Thompson had joined his friends Cad Pierce and Neil Kane. With the shotgun hooked over one elbow, he was calmly pouring whiskey into a glass.

"I don't want you to think," Vern Balance said, "that I don't appreciate what you did. My knees are still shaking." He included Pierce and Kane in his thanks, though he understood well enough that they had merely backed Ben Thompson, and otherwise would not likely have made any move at all.

Not answering, Thompson finished pouring and set the filled glass on the table. He pointed to the shimmering jewel of amber liquid. "*That's* what you really need, and you know it. You're tight as a spring; it would loosen you up. But, I guess there's no point in offering it."

"No," the other agreed, and Thompson tossed off the drink himself. Watching him, Balance went on, "I want you to know, I count myself under obligation. I intend to repay this."

Ben Thompson finished the drink, brushed a knuckle across his luxuriant mustache as he let his stare rest speculatively on the other man. "One never knows," he said briefly. "Maybe you can."

Balance left it at that.

Hearing his own name, as he crossed the lobby of the Drovers Cottage on the way to his room, Vern Balance halted and turned. The desk had been empty when he entered, but he saw that Lou Gore stood now in the half-open door behind it. As he went to her, she was frowning in a way that made him think, She's through putting up with me! This time, she's going to order me out of my room!

He was sure of it when she said icily, "Will you please step into the office? That is, if you have a minute."

"All right." He took off his hat as he moved around the counter; the woman pushed the door wide and drew aside for him to enter.

The office gave an illusion, at least, of being the coolest room in the hotel, because it was kept dark—the shades down, and drapes drawn part way across the windows. It was very much like walking into a cave. Vern Balance was at first only dimly aware of the heavy leather furniture, or the neat and polished square desk over against the windows. But he saw the person who rose slowly from a chair beside it; he halted stockstill, suddenly unaware of anything else.

When the door clicked shut behind him, he turned quickly to discover that, instead of following him in, Lou Gore had closed the two of them away in here, alone. Not moving from the threshold, he again faced Tess Spearman.

She looked as cool as the room, but there were traces of shock and sadness about her eyes that he had not seen there before. He said, "Believe me! This is Lou Gore's doing, not mine. I'm as surprised as you are."

"It was my doing," she corrected him; her voice, like her face, had changed—some of the life seemed gone from it. "We had the door open, talking, and I saw you cross the lobby. She couldn't understand when I asked her to call you in."

"I can't, myself," he said. "I know you've learned the truth about me, by now—your father said so. And I'd have thought I was the last person you'd be wanting to have in the same room with you!"

Tess lifted a hand, turned it and let it fall again. "I admit I'm—disappointed. I mean, that you never told me yourself. You had plenty of chances."

"I know. It comes of being a coward. That last time together, when we had our ride: I nearly made it then. But, I lost my nerve—and that's why you haven't seen me since."

In the near darkness of the room her eyes were little more than a shadow against her face. "You know how much I loved my brother," she said. "You know how I have to feel about the man who killed him! And yet—it's hard to believe there isn't *something* more to it, than what I've heard. I—I sort of thought I might be able to hear it from you."

"But what on earth can I tell you?" Balance demanded harshly. "That I was drunk the night it happened—and Bud Spearman, too? I don't think that helps much, does it."

She looked directly at him. "I'd like you to tell me exactly what happened. I promise to listen." And she seated herself again, and smoothed the skirt primly across her knees—an audience of one, frowning up at him expectantly. Vern Balance hesitated, and then lifted one shoulder in a shrug.

"All right—but I have to tell you, it doesn't make much sense to me, even yet." He remained standing: This was not going to be easy, but he thought he could say it better on his feet. "I do want to say, first of all, that I never was really a professional gambler. I was just footloose, and I guess irresponsible. I'd served an Army hitch, got discharged at Fort Leavenworth and simply drifted down to Abilene looking for excitement. But there *was* a professional card shark in that game, and he started deliberately throwing hands my way for some reason I've given up trying to understand.

"Bud Spearman, whatever else he might have been, was a very poor loser—especially, I guess, with a few drinks in him. He caught on to what was happening to him, and yelled that I was a cheat and went for his gun. Ernie Telford tried to calm him; but I didn't think Ernie was getting anywhere, and I lost my head and grabbed the first gun I could lay hands on. I still think I had some idea of making Bud drop his. But as I told you, I'd been drinking—I might add that I haven't done it since! My gun went off, somehow . . ."

It sounded lame enough. The girl waited a moment, as though to make sure he was finished. She looked again at the hands knotted together in her lap. "I—wanted to believe it was like that."

"Like what?"

"An accident."

"It's still a poor excuse!"

She had to nod agreement to that; but then her head came up and she said, with hesitant formality: "I do thank you, Mister Balance— for telling me. Of course, if Papa knew I'd gone behind his back . . ."

"He'll never know about it from me," Vern Balance assured her. "Only, I'm the one should thank *you*, for still wanting to hear my version—after I didn't have the courage to speak up, but left you instead to hear the story from someone else."

She didn't answer that, and he turned to go. But with his hand on the knob of the door he hesitated and looked back at her. "It's too much to hope, of course, that this makes any real difference."

"I don't know," she admitted slowly. "I don't know . . ."

He left her.

CHAPTER XIII

Friday, the fifteenth of August . . . another scorcher, perhaps the worst yet. The kind of day when you thought you could hear the timbers of Ellsworth's jimcrack buildings popping, as they sat and baked beneath the relentless sun. The kind of day when panting dogs flopped down anywhere and lay with tongues lolling and sides laboring so that it hurt to watch. The kind of day when bad tempers and long-festering grievances were apt to come to a head . . .

Toward midmorning a noisy argument broke out in the Oriental Palace and Balance left the office and went quickly to investigate. Billy Thompson, it seemed, had begun his day's drinking early. Lately he had been more or less behaving himself; but now, flushed and belligerent, he was trying to wrestle a whiskey bottle away from Monty, the day bartender. The latter, though sweating and scared, nevertheless kept a firm hold on it. "I'm sorry, Billy," he insisted. "Your brother give strict orders, nobody's to sell you more than a couple of drinks!"

No one made any move to interfere. John Sterling, the gambler, stood nearby toying with the bar dice, shaking and rolling them out upon the felt while he eyed Billy with an expression of cold dislike. Stepping up beside Thompson, Balance said, "Hello, Billy."

The man turned his head, without relinquishing his grip on the bottle. The blue eyes were bloodshot, the mouth loose beneath its mustache, but at least he seemed to be unarmed. Balance gave the bartender a nod. "Go get Ben."

Monty hurried away; Thompson, left in possession of the bottle, gave a grunt of victory and fumbled at a glass and filled it. Lifting the drink, he eyed Balance as though daring the latter to stop him.

Vern Balance, however, had no intention of getting involved in a family matter. He merely leaned an elbow on the bar and waited as

Billy drained off the whiskey, making a face as though it was the bitterest medicine; and now Ben came from the rear of the building with the bartender at his heels. Ben walked up behind his brother and he was plainly angry as he said, "All right—you've had enough." He took the bottle out of Billy's hand and set it on the counter; Vern Balance shoved it toward the bartender and it was quickly swept out of sight.

Ben put a hand on his brother's shoulder. "Come on, let's go on back. I got Neil Kane dealing monte; Cad's bucking his game."

With that he simply turned his brother from the bar and gave him a shove to get him started, and Billy walked away like an automaton.

Ben had a sour look and the bartender evidently misinterpreted it, for he said hurriedly, "Wasn't my fault, Ben. I never let him get like that; I only sold him the limit. But he was already in bad shape when he came in."

John Sterling spoke up, with no effort to hide the contempt in his voice. "He was in Lentz's, when I looked in there earlier. It struck me he was trying to work his way through every bar in town. I hope you keep an eye on him. He's got himself in trouble enough already."

Ben turned to look down the bar at the man. There was known to be no love lost between these two gamblers, Sterling being on too good terms with the town police. But just now Ben Thompson had business on his mind, and he said, "You might be interested in this game, John. Cad's got money and he wants to put up more than Neil is willing to cover. He asked me to find someone to take his over-bets."

Sterling's impassive features showed only a flicker of expression. "You throwing it to me, Ben? Hell, I'd like to take it—I feel lucky this morning. But I happen to be a little short."

Ben Thompson shrugged. "If *you* feel lucky, it ought to be good enough for anyone. I'll stake your play."

"I wonder why you don't take his bets yourself?"

"Like you said, I got to keep my eye on Billy. But if you want in the action, I'll back you."

Sterling set down the dice cup. "All right. Anything I should win, figure yourself in for half." Watching the pair of them start off toward the card room together, knowing how little liking these two had for each other, Vern Balance reflected that gambling could create as many strange alliances as politics.

Monty, behind the bar, said earnestly, "I got to thank you for stepping in when you did, Balance. That Bill Thompson! I don't mind saying he scares me. At least, I sure don't want to be the one to make him mad!"

Vern Balance nodded briefly, without answering, and now the half doors pushed open and Sheriff Whitney came in off the street. He had a concerned look and when Balance greeted him the sheriff nodded distractedly, searching the dim interior of the barroom. "Did I just see Ben Thompson in here?" And as Balance confirmed it: "Was Billy with him?"

"He's in back."

"How's he feeling?"

"Do you mean, is he sober? Afraid not." He added, "You sound worried."

The sheriff shook his head at the glass and bottle the houseman set out on the bar for him. "I'm always worried when I hear Billy Thompson's on the bottle! Anything can happen . . ."

"I don't think he's armed," Balance pointed out. "And now Ben's taken him under his wing. Ben can handle him." He didn't add, When Ben's sober, himself!

Whitney had brought out a handkerchief, and he mopped his fore-head and cheeks. "This heat!" he muttered. "Beats any summer I can remember! Mrs. Whitney and some friends had a picnic planned to-day, out at Howard's Grove—just to get away from town for a few hours. But when I heard about Billy falling off the wagon, just to be on the safe side I decided I'd best stick around. So I sent the family off without me."

"It's not your responsibility, Sheriff," Balance pointed out. "Even if there was to be trouble, it's a town matter."

The other shook his head as he put the handkerchief away. "The Thompson boys are friends of mine. I couldn't forgive myself if any-thing bad was to happen, when I might have been able to prevent it." He settled the hang of his coat, ran a palm across his bearded jaw. "Well, chances are I'm borrowing trouble. But, somehow I got a feeling . . ."

After he left, Balance found himself disturbed by the sheriff's premonitions, in spite of himself; but when he walked back for a look at the action in the card room, things looked peaceful enough. The game was progressing. A bottle was going the rounds but Billy Thompson, at least, wasn't drinking—he had gone to sleep, sprawled in a chair in a corner. The others in the room were watching Cad Pierce buck Kane's monte game and to Balance it was a demonstration of the old truth that there were few less profitable pastimes. Kane was too good at manipulating the three card spread, and his friend probably too blear-eyed to follow his movements. The more he lost, the more recklessly he plunged. The greenbacks were piling up in front of Kane, and on every call John Sterling was there as well, to collect his share.

Ben Thompson was checking his arsenal, as a craftsman regularly examines the tools of his trade—in his case, a revolver and a Winchester rifle that he kept in the closet built especially to house them, as well as the twin-barreled English shotgun Cad Pierce had given him on another occasion when the Texan had been flush and trying to get rid of his money. Balance considered telling Thompson about his talk with the sheriff, then decided there was no point in it. He turned back instead to the office.

Glennon had come in and was at his desk, going through some mail. There was nothing really for Balance to do, so after a word with his partner he got his hat and left for the Drovers Cottage. There he had a meal of sorts, for which he felt little appetite, and then went up to his room and stripped off his outer clothing.

Stretched out on the bed, staring at the heated air beneath the ceiling, he found himself reluctantly playing out again, for perhaps the hundredth time, that scene two days ago in the office downstairs—remembering every word that had been spoken, every inflection of Tess Spearman's voice as she discussed her brother's death: *I wanted to believe it was like that—an accident* . . . Once more, futilely, he asked himself just what she might have meant.

He simply couldn't afford to read too much into it.

Balance had seen the Spearmans together—father and daughter— just once, yesterday, for the briefest of encounters out in the second story corridor. Meeting them at the head of the stairs he had halted, ready to speak; but old Clayt, limping on his walking stick, had tightened his grip on his daughter's arm and his ravaged face closed like a fist. The two had swept by without a word, only a fleeting touch of the girl's look meeting his for an instant with an expression he could not hope to interpret.

If he could just manage to keep anyone from collecting the bounty offered for him by Clayt Spearman, he told himself bleakly, he would be better off never even to think again of any member of that family . . .

He dozed, presently, and woke drenched in his own sweat, his brain dulled and drugged by the heat. He sat up on the edge of the bed, knuckling his scalp, and for almost the first time since the night of Bud Spearman's death felt a sudden, piercing need for a drink. He thought about that for a minute, a little appalled at himself. But then he said, aloud, "No." He hauled his boots to him, pulled them on, and then went over to the wash basin to soak his head and clear the fog of sleep from it.

When he walked out of the hotel lobby, the heat felt dense and almost solid—like being packed in cotton wool that cramped the muscles of the chest and restricted breathing. And stepping from the shadow of the gallery, he actually cringed under the full, smashing weight of the sun. Toward three o'clock, he judged—the hottest time of day, and the hottest day of the summer. He thought of Sheriff Whitney's family and friends, fleeing the town for the hoped-for relief of a day in Howard's Grove a few miles east of Ellsworth. Dryly he thought, I hope they're enjoying themselves . . .

The galleries fronting the line of buildings along South Main formed a tunnel, whose dense shadow was almost impenetrable after the white, brittle sunlight; he was almost face to face with Ben Thompson, on the walk in front of Beebe's store, before they saw each other. Balance sensed at once that Thompson was furiously angry, even before the Texan demanded, "You seen Johnny Sterling?"

"I haven't seen anybody. I've been asleep in my room."

"Somebody just told me he might have gone into Nick Lentz's," Thompson said. "I've already been there but I figure to take another look." He added grimly, "If he's in this town—I'll find him!"

"What's wrong?" Balance demanded. "Why do you want him?"

"The damned welsher! You were there—you heard our deal, on Cad Pierce's overbets."

Balance answered cautiously. "I remember you talking. You were to back him, for half of anything he won . . ."

"He took close to a thousand off of Cad—and then, when I was out of the room for a minute, he pocketed the money and left. That was over an hour ago. He's been ducking me ever since."

Vern Balance pointed out, "Maybe it's only a mistake. Surely the man would have better sense?" In a gambler's decalogue there was no graver sin.

"Well, we'll see damned quick," Ben Thompson promised darkly, "if he's in Lentz's. I want you with me," he added. "You're my witness to the deal."

Balance was reluctant, but he owed a favor or two to Ben Thompson and he nodded. "All right."

Lentz's saloon stood one door west of Beebe's. When they entered, the first thing Vern Balance saw was Sterling and Happy Jack Morco, together at the bar with a bottle and glasses between them, and their wary glances trained on the street entrance.

Ben Thompson halted in midstride and Balance saw him stiffen; he himself had held up just inside the entrance, cautiously watchful as the swinging panels clacked and went still behind him. And Thompson said sharply, "What the hell, Morco! Are you in this?"

The men at the bar exchanged a look. "I don't know what you're talking about," the deputy retorted. "Nothing's happened that I know of . . . unless you come in here to start it."

"Your friend knows what I'm talking about!" Thompson said, and switched his cold regard to John Sterling. "Where's the money that belongs to me?"

Sterling's eyes held the shine of the whiskey he had been drinking. "I don't owe you anything." His speech was a little slurred.

"Then why are you hiding?" Thompson snapped. He stabbed a pointing finger. "I'll give you one minute. Then I want to see that money counted out and lying on the bar!"

The gambler's sallow cheeks had blanched of color. Suddenly, without any warning he bawled an obscenity and strode forward, his arm swinging. Whether it was a fist or the flat of his hand that struck

Thompson on the cheek, Vern Balance was never sure. But he heard it hit, saw his friend's head jerk with the blow; and then, before Ben Thompson could make any answering move, Happy Jack Morco's revolver was out of the holster and pointed straight at his chest.

"All right, you bastard!" the deputy cried. "You been asking for this. If you want it now, go right ahead. I'd just love to see you try something!"

Thompson's face had turned livid with rage, but the gun caught him up and held him motionless while, through the room, a hush fell as men broke off whatever they were doing.

Vern Balance had a hand thrust inside his coat, toward his own weapon. He thought the deputy must surely have known Ben Thompson was unarmed, to have dared draw against him. Now the Texan's shoulders lifted and settled; when he spoke his voice held a tremor.

"Morco, I've already taken too damned much off of you—that tin badge you wear gave me no choice; but you're pushing too hard now! I don't allow scum to pull a gun on me. Or lay hands on me, either!" And the weight of his glare shifted to Happy Jack's companion.

John Sterling blinked back at him; he showed signs of being a trifle abashed at the thought of what he had done. Morco, however, was as arrogant as ever. "Big talk!" he sneered. "But you aren't throwing your weight around with *me,* Thompson!"

"No?" Ben Thompson looked askance at the gun, and there was icy scorn in his voice as he said, "Have you really got nerve enough to pull that trigger?" When Morco, for whatever reason, gave no answer, Thompson dismissed him. "Just don't think you're getting away with anything," he told John Sterling. "Because nobody welshes on Ben Thompson!"

And he turned on his heels and walked out of there, Vern Balance falling into place behind him. At the last minute, Happy Jack Morco yelled hoarsely, "Go on—get out!"

But he had waited too long. The result was distinctly one of anti-climax.

Minutes later, in the Oriental Palace, Balance watched and thought he could never have seen a man so angry.

With Thompson, you judged by a kind of cold ferocity that he exuded, a restless energy that made it impossible for him to settle.

The main room was almost empty now except for the Thompsons and their friends, Neil Kane and Cad Pierce, sharing a table with a bottle and glasses in front of them; Ben, for his part, paced the room like some caged animal, cursing and raging, interrupting himself only to pour another shot and toss it down.

"Hell!" Billy Thompson spoke with drunken belligerence. "The Thompsons don't have to take this off anybody! Let me have a gun, and the two of us will go clean up on 'em."

His brother looked at him. "The shape you're in? That's one thing that *won't* happen! Whatever is done, *I'll* do it—understand?" The younger man scowled but dropped his eyes, apparently knowing better than to argue with Ben in such a mood.

It was at that moment that boots trampled the dry plankings outside the door and a voice bawled into the stillness: "Texas sonsabitches! *Come out here and fight!*"

For an instant no one moved; then, grim of face, Vern Balance strode to the door. A look across the batwings, and he was turning his head with a quick warning: "It's Sterling, and Morco. They're armed to the teeth!"

A chair clattered as the men in the room scrambled to their feet. Cad Pierce had caught Ben Thompson's arm and was arguing with him—Balance heard him say, "Don't be a fool, Ben! Against a badge, you lose whatever way it comes out!" But Thompson shook him off —wild-eyed with rage, past listening to anyone's advice. Balance didn't hesitate. Not giving himself time to think of consequences, he slipped his gun from the holster and shouldered out through the slotted doors, to face the pair beneath the gallery.

Somewhere they had promoted a shotgun for Sterling, an extra sixshooter for Happy Jack. They were both just drunk enough to make them dangerous. Morco, hat missing and the sweat shining on his face, brandished one of his weapons and shouted, "We don't want you, Balance! Send that Thompson bastard out here—or else stand aside while we come in and get him!"

"I'll do neither," Balance said. "I warned you to stay away from here."

"*You* was warned too, mister!"

"About going against the law?" Balance shook his head. "Not this time! You're drunk, and for private reasons bent on turning a respectable place of business into a shooting gallery. Come one step closer and I'll be justified to put a bullet in you!" And he raised the gun and took deliberate aim, sighting squarely on Morco's scowling face.

He had the satisfaction of seeing Happy Jack's flushed cheeks turn muddy with alarm. It sent the man back a step, but he still had bluster in him; loudly enough to be heard within the Palace, he cried, "I'll settle with you later. Right now, you tell Thompson and any of his friends that's got the guts to meet us, we're waiting!" Turning, he stumbled against his companion, staggered briefly; then both men were headed noisily off along the boardwalk, back the way they had come.

When he was sure, Vern Balance pushed through the half doors to find the bartender, and Kane and Pierce, looking at him without expression. Ben and Billy Thompson were missing. The door at the rear of the room stood open, telling where they had disappeared to; Balance started after them.

He was met in the doorway by Joe Glennon, wearing a puzzled scowl and holding the steel pen that he had forgotten to put down. "What's going on?" the fat man exclaimed. "What got into them Thompsons, the way they came stampeding through here?"

"Where are they?" For answer he got a jerk of the head toward the alley door; it stood open, against the white blast of sunlight. As Balance shouldered past, he heard his partner saying, "Sounded like they were at that closet where Ben keeps his guns . . ."

Balance got a glimpse of it—the unlocked door, the empty interior. After that he was in the alley and squinting against the glare as he hastily looked about him. At once he saw the Thompsons, heading west at a run along the rear of the buildings. Ben had his rifle and a six-shooter; a few paces behind, Billy was hurrying to catch up, sunlight bouncing smears of light off the twin barrels of the weapon he carried—it was his brother's English-made, breech-loading shotgun. As Balance watched, they turned into the passageway separating a couple of these crackerbox structures that fronted on South Main; and then they were gone.

He swung about, shaking his head, and as he re-entered the building he again confronted Joe Glennon. This time he answered his partner's questions: "Ben Thompson's having trouble with a man who tried to renege on a gambling deal. Ben put his weight on him; but the man's a friend of Morco's and Morco must have decided on a showdown."

"That's plain madness!"

Balance shrugged. "Well, it's the hottest day of the year and they've all been drinking. I guess, sometime or other, this had to come to a head."

"Then, let it!" said Glennon. "So long as they take their fight somewhere else."

"You talk as though what happens to the Thompsons was none of our business."

"Do you make it to be?"

That got him a look of disgust from his partner but, instead of arguing, Balance brushed past him and hurried on through the building, anxious to see what was happening out front in the plaza.

Of Morco and Sterling there was no sign at all—he thought they might have returned to Nick Lentz's, and their drinking. But now, as he stood waiting in the heat trapped beneath the wooden awning, he saw Ben Thompson appear from between two buildings farther along the block with Billy, right behind him, drunkenly brandishing the shotgun in a way to make Balance think, My God, I hope he hasn't got it cocked!

Scarcely had the idea crossed his mind when one barrel let go, a startling smash of sound in the quiet. Billy was staggered, the shotgun all but torn from his grasp by the unexpected explosion; a couple of Texans, passing, yelled out and dived for safety as the charge of buckshot struck the sidewalk planking almost under their feet. And Ben Thompson whirled, and Balance saw him angrily snatch the weapon from his brother's hands.

Standing there in the sun, he tucked his rifle under an arm and broke the shotgun. He was working to render it harmless by removing the shells, but seeming to be having trouble with them; and now the doors of Lentz's saloon burst open. Sterling and Morco came lunging out, and the town marshal, Brocky Jack Norton, was close at their heels. Balance saw the guns in their hands; almost without thinking, he yelled, "Ben! *Watch out!*"

There had been little enough activity on the plaza before, and now it emptied itself as if by magic. Boots pounded the sidewalks, doors slammed; Balance saw a couple of men head for cover behind a boxcar that stood on the weedy siding.

Ben Thompson had no more time to give to the shotgun. Quickly thrusting it back into his brother's hands, he turned and started at a run out into the center of the plaza; Billy floundered after him, tripped and nearly went sprawling. Vern Balance saw Thompson's purpose when he halted near the west end of the depot and there took up his position—in the open, where wild shots would do the least damage. Rifle barrel a smear of sunlight, and Billy reeling uncertainly at his elbow, he called his challenge to the men in front of Lentz's: "You really think you want a fight? You can have it—any time you want to start!"

But they suddenly appeared in no hurry.

Hurling drunken threats had been one thing; actually facing Ben Thompson out in the naked, open plaza would be a different matter. Balance could hear Morco and Sterling and the marshal furiously arguing. Now Thompson's friends, Cad Pierce and Neil Kane, stepped out beside him, under the Palace's arcade. Vern Balance demanded, "What do you think we should do?"

"Stay out of this," Kane answered promptly; and Cad Pierce added, "It's Ben's affair. He wouldn't want us interfering."

"But—" He let it go, with a shake of the head. These two should know, but he still felt strongly a debt he owed Ben Thompson for intervening that day the men of Rafter 7 had had him cold. And Happy Jack, after all, was a common foe . . .

Then Balance saw the sheriff.

He hadn't noticed when Cap Whitney joined the group in front of Lentz's, but now he had left there and started walking toward the depot; he turned back briefly when Marshal Norton shouted after him, "Damn it, I said this is a town matter. Ain't nothing for you to deal with."

"I don't see *you* dealing with it," the sheriff retorted. "Those Thompsons are friends of mine; they won't give me trouble. I'll take them into Glennon's, and buy them a drink, and this whole thing will blow over—if you don't let some idiot stir it up again!" And he swung about and went plodding across the sun-shimmering plaza—a slight, bareheaded figure, clearly unarmed.

Ben stepped forward to meet him, Billy still at his heels, and they talked. Ben Thompson seemed to be arguing, and Whitney answered. Balance saw him lay a hand on Ben's shoulder in a friendly gesture; the other shrugged it off, but the lawman put it back again, talking earnestly, and this time Ben let it stay. After another moment the sheriff placed himself in the middle, between the two brothers, and deftly he turned them in the direction of the Oriental Palace.

Cad Pierce said shortly, "Well! It looks like Whitney called off the war. I figured Ben had gone past that point."

Vern Balance found he had been holding his breath. He let trapped air from his lungs. "I don't know if it's called off," he said, "or only postponed." But trouble did seem to be averted, at least for the moment. He turned back into the saloon, leaving Kane and Pierce outside to wait for the Thompsons.

Billy entered first, weaving and still clutching the shotgun, his eyes glazed with the whiskey shine. The sheriff, a step behind him, clearly showed the strain of what he had just been through: His cheeks were ashen and runneled with sweat, but his voice went on—soothing and unhurried, continuing to push cool common sense at the angry pair. The batwings pulsed once more and now Ben paused a moment in the doorway. His face appeared thunderous with the temper that was even yet, Balance judged, barely held on leash.

At that moment Neil Kane, still outside, shouted: "Get out here, Ben! *They're coming with guns!*"

Ben Thompson swore savagely as he jerked about and shouldered through the door again, heedless of Cap Whitney's quick protest. Balance caught the latter's grimace of despair, as he saw his efforts gone to waste; but without hesitation the sheriff turned to follow. And Billy, as though towed by a string, wheeled around mechanically and stumbled after them.

Balance was only a step behind. Over Billy's shoulder, he glimpsed Happy Jack Morco running toward them, brandishing a six-shooter —he must have had some drunken idea of putting his shot into Ben

Thompson's back while it was turned. Now instead he saw Ben coming to meet him, the Winchester leveled for action. Morco at once put on the brakes; he yelled something, his voice splitting in fear. He was trying to backpedal, and nearly losing his footing, when Ben Thompson fired.

The forward stride threw off Ben's aim and the bullet ate wood from the door casing of Beebe's mercantile, right at Happy Jack's elbow. The latter cried out again. Unhurt, but with his own six-shooter completely forgotten, he lurched aside and made a blind, diving scramble through the doorway, ignominiously hunting cover. Ben continued to stride forward, working the rifle's lever, apparently intent on making a finish; he seemed unaware of Sheriff Whitney at his back, exclaiming hoarsely, "Ben! You're making a mistake! You hear me? Don't push this . . ."

Now Vern Balance's view was blocked by Billy Thompson, still trailing the others with the English shotgun in his fists. Suddenly Billy had halted and was lifting the weapon, trying to draw wavering aim on the only target in sight. Past his shoulder Balance saw the sheriff glance around, caught the look on Whitney's face as he saw the shotgun pointed at him. Frantically he tried to get out of the way but Billy, swaying drunkenly, swung the weapon to match his move. And then, even as Balance reached to grab him, the gun went off with a blast that was ear-punishing, trapped beneath the arcade's wooden awning.

Vern Balance slowly lowered his arm, staring in horror. The sheriff had doubled forward as the charge hit him; somehow he pulled himself erect—his whole left side bloodied and ghastly, the lifeless arm hanging in shreds. His lips moved and then, slowly, he crumpled and slid down the wall of the store at his back.

CHAPTER XIV

Ben Thompson was the first to move. He got to his brother and he snatched the smoking shotgun out of his hands, Billy being too drunk to prevent him. Ben's face was terrible. "You dumb bastard!" he cried. "You've shot our best friend!"

It was doubtful if Billy understood, even yet, just what he had done. Vern Balance heard him mutter something that sounded like, "I'd of shot if it was Jesus Christ himself . . ." Then, shoving past the brothers, Balance got to the stricken sheriff and dropped to a knee beside him.

Whitney wasn't dead. Eyes dilated, face white with shock and pain, he somehow managed to force out words: "Billy didn't mean to! It was an accident." And then: "Send—send for my wife . . ."

Balance, nodding hastily, had to turn and shout angrily at the men who were beginning to crowd about them. "Damn it, give him air! His whole left side is riddled! Somebody fetch a doctor . . ."

Those next minutes were too occupied with the wounded sheriff for him to think of other things. Since someone had to take charge, Balance did. One man was dispatched for a doctor, while four others were detailed to rig up some kind of stretcher—no more danger would be involved in trying to move Whitney, he thought, than in leaving him lying here amid the heat and flies and filth of the passage between the buildings. Balance's first thought was to have him carried into the Oriental Palace; but then John Montgomery was there, to point out that his brother-in-law's home was a mere two blocks away. Surely the best place for him was his own bed.

Then Balance remembered the sheriff's wife, and the picnic at Howard's Grove six miles east of town; he found someone willing to saddle up and make the ride to summon her. And now at last, with all this tended to, Vern Balance had his first moment since the shotgun blast to catch his breath, look around and see how things were going with the Thompsons.

It was like a look into a cauldron.

Ellsworth might almost have been deserted, a quarter hour ago when they faced their enemies in the blistering silence of the plaza; now the place seethed with activity. He heard shouting, saw several men streaming on foot across toward the north side of the tracks where, for the moment, excitement appeared to have shifted. He saw Joe Glennon in front of the Palace and went to him. "What's going on? Where are the Thompsons?"

The fat man was bareheaded, sweating profusely; he looked vaguely frightened. He pointed to the far side of the plaza. "Ben walked over there, a while ago. I don't know where Billy disappeared to. Did I hear right? Did he kill the sheriff?"

"Whitney's bad hit. He's alive but I don't know if he'll pull through or not."

Glennon swore with feeling. "I heard somebody say the Texans are holed up in the Grand Central, daring the whole town to make a fight of it. God knows where this can lead!"

Balance said, "I'll see what I can find out."

He started across the plaza, walking briskly, hearing a murmur of crowd noise but blocked by the sprawling depot from a view of what might be happening beyond. Suddenly the sound of a horse came up behind him, at a hard lope; he turned quickly and saw Billy Thompson riding across the open, flailing the animal with his heels. Billy kept his sorrel in the stable behind the Grand Central—it occurred to Balance that one of the Thompsons' many Texas friends must have gone after it, put on saddle and gear and taken it to wherever Billy had been hiding since he gunned the sheriff.

Balance shouted as he went by, but he gave no sign of hearing. A shoe iron struck a ringing note from steel as the horse crossed the tracks. Then Billy rounded a corner of the depot, out of sight—but Balance heard the swelling of angry yells that greeted him. Minutes later, Vern Balance cleared the station corner and the line of buildings that was North Main spread itself out in front of him.

A time or two, in prison, he had seen something like this—lines drawn, the yard breaking into factions and the men standing about motionless and yet exuding a danger that was more frightening than any uproar. So it was in this sunstruck heart of Ellsworth, where now Kansas and Texas—North and South—stood face to face. Accident or not, it looked as though the shooting of Sheriff Whitney had been enough to break the uneasy truce. Balance thought there must be close to a hundred men here, with more arriving constantly; he wondered if riders could be out, alerting the trail-herd camps to a showdown in the making. In defiance of the ordinances both groups bristled with guns, that shot back shimmering glints of reflected light toward the hot sky; everyone seemed intent on what was happening in front of the Grand Central.

The brick hotel stood at the head of a slight embankment, behind a line of a half dozen spindly trees set out in latticed boxes, and drooping limply in the August heat. The Texans did appear to have taken over. Balance saw Neil Kane, Cad Pierce, other cronies of the Thompsons in the group crowding the limestone sidewalk; and there was Billy Thompson, who had reined in and was leaning from the saddle in heated conference with his brother.

They were quarreling furiously—from Ben's gestures, and Billy's emphatic headshakes, Balance could only guess that Ben wanted the younger man to leave town but that Billy was resisting. After what he did, Balance thought, if he *doesn't* go—and that damned quick!—even Ben can't stop this town from tearing him to pieces . . .

A townsman yelled something that made Billy whip around as though he meant to turn his horse and charge the hostile crowd. Ben grabbed his rein and held it firmly, while the sorrel moved nervously about and the dust rose under its hoofs; after a moment's further lecturing, he must have cut through the fog of whiskey-meanness and made his brother see reason. In any event, Billy seemed to nod agreement. He gave the sorrel a kick, tearing it free of Ben's grasp. He jumped it down the embankment and started off eastward along the tracks; but even as he rode, his head was turned to hurl drunken taunts and obscenities at his foes. Infuriated, they surged forward.

Ben Thompson had broken the shotgun and was feeding fresh shells into it. He quickly slapped the barrels into place and stepped out on the embankment, the weapon leveled. "Stay back!" he warned loudly. "Anybody that wants to stop him, will have to go through me!"

That held them, although someone yelled, "Damn it, the man's a murderer!"

"Nobody's died yet," Ben retorted. "And I'm sure as hell not letting any Kansas mob lay hands on him!" Ranged solidly behind him, the Texans stood ready to give their support. And so the two groups faced each other, bristling with guns and barely leashed violence as Billy Thompson rode out of Ellsworth.

To Vern Balance, watching it all from his place near the depot, it appeared that the Texans had won for the moment; but he knew nothing was really settled. Now there seemed to be new activity in front of Larkin's store, just opposite. He saw a number of townspeople that he recognized, and on an impulse he crossed over there.

The realtor, James Miller—the Mayor of Ellsworth, was speaking in a voice that had been trained to carry. It looked as though he must have been called away from his supper table—he was in shirtsleeves, bareheaded, and a napkin dangled forgotten between two buttons of his waistcoat. He was haranguing Marshal Norton and the other officers, who stood glowering but plainly had little to offer in rebuttal. "What kind of a police force is this?" Miller was raving, beside himself. "You let that fellow ride away, bold as brass, and I didn't notice a one of you doing anything!"

The marshal and his deputies exchanged uneasy glances. Face pale under the tongue-lashing, Norton said, "But you can see how many there are of those Texans. They got completely out of hand."

"And whose job was it supposed to be to prevent that?" the mayor retorted. "I'm going to give you one more chance: Get out there and disarm those people. You can start with Ben Thompson. I want him put under arrest!"

"Arrest Thompson?" the marshal echoed, as though disbelieving his ears; and Ed Hogue, one of the deputies, cried hoarsely, "Hell, man! I ain't committing suicide!"

"By God, you're fired!" Miller cried then, and his voice trembled. He had discovered the napkin hanging from his waistcoat; he snatched it free and wadded it and flung it furiously to the ground. "The whole, white-livered lot of you!"

"What are you doing?" The druggist, Ward Linker, looked frightened out of his skin. "You've just gone and left Ellsworth without any kind of law enforcement!"

The mayor thrust this aside with an angry gesture. "Some people have tried to tell me the kind we had was worse than none at all. Maybe I should have listened! Here we are, on the verge of starting the War all over again, right here on the streets of Ellsworth—and nobody in sight with any idea how to prevent it!" A distraught and frightened man, he turned his back on Linker's protests and on the men he had fired—and came face to face with Vern Balance.

The latter said quickly, "Maybe I can do something. Ben's being pushed pretty hard, but I don't really think he wants to fight the whole town. Let me talk to him."

"You!" Linker snorted. "You're no better than that Texas riffraff, your own self!"

Balance only looked at him. But the mayor was scowling thoughtfully.

There was a nervous tic jumping in one cheek as Miller glanced again at the sullen quartet of policemen he had had to fire; he drew a breath and when he spoke his voice was edged with strain. "If there's anything you can do," he told Balance, "then for God's sake do it! Because if somebody don't—this town could blow apart!"

Balance nodded curtly. Not giving anyone time for a change of mind, he heeled about and started toward the Grand Central.

The sidewalk was clogged with townsmen who got in his way; he shouldered roughly through them and then the cross street lay empty before him and he went on alone through the sunglare. With the Texas faction in front of the hotel waiting and watching him come, he would not let any faltering in his stride show how vulnerable he suddenly felt. He kept walking, in a dead silence that made audible the grind of street dust beneath the soles of his shoes, and more than one gun barrel was pointed at him among that silent group.

And then Ben Thompson was there, the shotgun hung in the bend of one arm. The gambler's face was unreadable as Balance halted before him. "I saw you talking to the city fathers," he said coldly. "Are you their errand boy now?"

The man had changed; Vern Balance felt chilled by his stare, already doubtful that anything would come of this. "I deserve better from you, Ben," he said. "I thought we were friends."

Not answering that, the other demanded, "What's the word on Cap Whitney?"

"Still alive, the last I heard. No thanks to Billy."

"He never meant to shoot him. It was an accident."

"He was falling-down drunk!" Balance retorted. "Does that excuse him?"

Thompson's expression altered subtly. Suddenly he looked tired and discouraged. "I guess it was my fault, if anybody's. I should have taken the damned gun away from him, and kept it out of his hands. But, I didn't manage. Things were happening too fast."

Balance shook his head. "You can't always protect him, Ben," he pointed out quietly. "After all, what is he now—twenty-six?" The others lips tightened. Vern Balance went on: "I told the mayor I'd try to help find a way to cool off this business before more blood gets spilled—by mistake, or otherwise."

"Do you see any way?" Thompson demanded harshly. "It's got nothing to do with the town. It's between me and Happy Jack Morco. Morco's finally declared war. You can't expect me to walk away from it, just because he uses his police badge to hide behind."

"Morco's no longer wearing his badge. He's been fired."

That came as a complete surprise. "You're joshing me!"

"It's the truth. Not only him, but the whole police force—Miller's wiped the board clean."

The Texan's mouth shaped a soundless whistle. "That's *one* thing I sure as hell hadn't counted on!" On a sudden decision he added, "All right. Because I trust *you,* you can tell the mayor I said this: If he'll guarantee to disarm Morco and John Sterling, and put them both under peace bond—then I'll hand over my own guns. I don't say I think it will do any good. But I'm willing to go along."

Vern Balance felt an easing of tension, as he heard this. He hesitated, looking at Ben Thompson's companions. "What about them?"

"They're only here to back my play," Thompson assured him. "They no more want a showdown than I do—unless of course it's forced on us." Suddenly, surprisingly, he tossed the shotgun, caught it by the breech and offered it, stock-first. "Here," he said gruffly.

"Take this." He slipped the revolver from his holster. "And this . . . Show these to the mayor—they ought to prove whether I'm in earnest. But if Morco and his tinhorn friend won't follow suit, then I hold you to see that I get these back. You understand?"

Balance studied the man. To give up his guns at such a time would be, for someone like Ben Thompson, a drastic concession. Dimly he perceived that it was, after all, a gesture made out of friendship —simply because Thompson trusted him, and because Vern Balance had laid his own integrity on the line, in pledging himself to an effort to keep the peace.

"I understand," he said, and accepted the weapons. "I don't see what more Miller can ask from you . . ."

Back again, then, across the empty street, feeling the silent stares that met him and hearing the murmurs of speculation that rose in his wake as he passed. At Larkin's, no one had moved, no one had done anything. Now, at sight of the shotgun, the mayor stammered, "What—what did he say?"

"He's willing to be reasonable," Balance answered bluntly. "As I tried to tell you all along. He's giving up his weapons on condition that these two do the same." And he nodded to Morco and Sterling.

He thought Miller actually turned pale with relief. But instantly Happy Jack Morco swelled with anger and, he suspected, a trace of fear. "No!"

"By God, yes!" The shotgun snapped level in Balance's grip; there was a scramble as men on either side of Morco and the gambler moved hastily out of the way. Balance had lost all his patience; tightly he said, "You two know as well as I do, you're the real cause of everything that's happened. Now, hand over those guns—don't tempt me to finish it right here!"

Morco's black eyes locked with his own and he read almost a crazy hatred in them. But John Sterling appeared to have sobered; with no expression at all in his gambler's face, he flipped open his coat and plucked the long-barreled Colt from behind his waistband, and Miller quickly accepted it. At that, seeing himself left alone, Happy Jack Morco could do nothing else but comply. He turned over his six-shooter, wordlessly, and with a fierce scowl swung around and strode away from there. And when Balance looked again for

John Sterling he discovered that the gambler had already vanished.

He eased the trapped breath from his lungs, and let the shotgun pivot around his trigger finger and extended it, stock first. "Take care of these," he said coldly as the mayor took Ben Thompson's weapons from him. "He's going to expect them back in good condition."

As Balance went to make his report to the Texans still clustered before the Grand Central, a noisy posse of townsmen was already forming to ride out in pursuit of Billy Thompson. Drunk or sober, Balance was willing to wager they would likely turn back before they ran any real risk of catching up with him . . .

CHAPTER XV

By eight o'clock, that night of August 15, the Ellsworth police force had been reinstated.

It was done at a stormy special session of the city council, over a protest from member Jim Gore of the Drovers Cottage. All the police who had been fired were voted back into office, with the sole exception of Marshal Norton himself who, apparently, had been chosen for the scapegoat; in his place Ed Hogue—one of the deputies, who had also served briefly as under-sheriff to the wounded Cap Whitney—was promoted to the top job. Happy Jack Morco was on hand, along with the others, to pin the badge again to his vest and pick up the gun that had been taken from him. And as he did so, he let a triumphant and hating look travel to the back of the room where Vern Balance stood with his shoulders against the wall, appalled at this latest turn of events.

It, of course, nullified the terms of truce offered by Ben Thompson; but having got over their terror of a few short hours ago, the council was riding a high saddle again and Balance knew, from bitter experience, how useless it would be to argue. So he held his tongue, merely listening in disbelief as Ward Linker declared loudly: "And now *that's* been settled, I want to offer a resolution abolishing the Texas cattle trade from Ellsworth."

That loosed a storm, that the mayor finally quelled with the banging of the inkwell he used for a gavel. Jim Gore was on his feet. "Like what Abilene did?" he shouted. "Is that what you want, Linker? Deliberately cut our own throats?"

"Don't try to scare me with Abilene," the drugstore owner retorted. "Getting rid of Texas cattle was the smartest thing they ever did. They saved their town!"

"They nearly killed it! Don't forget, I was there—I saw how close they came. And remember, Ellsworth doesn't have any other income yet to fill the gap, the way Abilene had. Without the Texans, just what do you intend to live on?"

Two other council members, speaking at once, tried to answer him, and Miller had to use the inkwell again. "For God's sake, let's try to hold onto our tempers!" the mayor exclaimed. "There's too much at stake here. Personally I'm in favor of the resolution, though I wasn't really sure until today. Just how many more shootings is it going to take to convince us?"

"I got a word I'd like to put in," someone called out from the crowded benches, and a man rose to his feet. A fine white mane of hair glinted in the lamplight as Clayt Spearman, leaning on his cane, ran a cold stare over the faces that surrounded him.

"I'm an outsider here," he admitted, and the sound of Texas in his voice was enough to prove it. "But I speak for some that I figure have a right to be heard—and I'm gonna tell you-all a few things, whether you like it or not! You talk big about getting rid of the Texans. Well, what if the shoe happens to be on the other foot? It ever occur to anyone in these pipsqueak Kansas towns, that we got no great love for you, either?

"You-all need our business—and yet, bar Jim Gore and maybe one or two others, men like you that run Ellsworth think it's all right to treat us and our crews as though we was something less than dirt!"

"Damn little business we've had out of you, *this* summer!" someone said. "And even less hard cash . . ."

"We ain't to blame for that!" Clayt Spearman retorted. "The whole country's in trouble! All we've asked was a little patience . . . but, believe me, our patience with *you* is about gone! You gouge us with your prices, you cheat our crews and turn the trash you call a police force loose on them!

"There's been fault on both sides," he went on, not letting anyone break in. "I hold no brief for killers like Ben and Billy Thompson; and I guess it's common knowledge how things stand between me and their friend Balance. Kick 'em all out of Ellsworth and you'll hear no complaint from me. But if you got any concern for your town, you'll send *this* murdering scum back to California—where he came from!" And the cane lifted, and pointed at Happy Jack Morco.

The latter's face, under its rooster comb of stiff brown hair, darkened with fury. "Why, you old bastard! I don't have to take that!"

Ignoring him, Clayt Spearman went right on. "Because, I'm telling you: The *next* time he takes it in his head to run wild like he done today—you may have more trouble on your hands than you know how to deal with!"

"Hear, hear!" cried Jim Gore, slapping the table with the flat of a hand.

The mayor rapped for silence. He seemed to be having difficulty holding his voice steady. "If you don't mind, Mister Spearman," he said stiffly, "I'm afraid we have to solve our town's problems as we see best."

"Suit yourselves." From his coat pocket the old man brought out a sheet of yellow paper. "Still, I thought you might like to know about the wire I just got from a reliable source in Chicago. According to this, it looks like there might be a break in the market at last. But then, I guess you-all ain't interested," he went on, with heavy sarcasm. "You can just believe I'll be passing the word among my friends, about the talk I heard here tonight. If Ellsworth don't want our trade, I know other drovers besides myself that are of a mind to pick up and tote our herds to Newton, or Wichita, or any other place at all where we can do business in peace—and not get harassed by the scum you call law officers!"

Happy Jack Morco cursed him savagely; Ward Linker was shouting, "It's nothing but a bluff!"

"Suit yourselves," Spearman said again. He was through arguing. He stuffed the telegram back into his pocket, as he turned away with a summoning nod to Ernie Telford who had been seated next to him. And the old man came stumping up the aisle, leaning heavily on his cane, disdainfully oblivious to the hubbub of angry voices that rose behind him.

It brought him face to face with Vern Balance.

They had met only once since the night of the lynching attempt, on the riverbank. Now, confronted, the old Texan's eyes glared their hatred; Balance merely parried the look as he said earnestly, "You talked sense to them. I hope they have the sense to listen."

Clayt Spearman gave no reaction, no sign that he had heard. It was big Ernie Telford, looming behind his employer, who spoke with a hard sneer quirking his lips. "I wonder. Now that Ben Thompson's handed over his guns, you might start getting a little anxious."

"About somebody collecting that five hundred?" Balance replied, his own face carefully expressionless. "As far as Ben Thompson's concerned, the deal he made is off since Morco's reinstated; Jim Gore will see to it Ben gets his weapons back. But if you're thinking about the bounty, Telford, don't let Thompson stop you. I can keep him out of it—and I will."

He wasn't sure, but he thought those other eyes lost a little of their boldness, before the direct challenge. "I'll bet!" was all Ernie Telford said. And then Clayt Spearman had turned and brushed past, without having spoken a word in acknowledgment of the man who had killed his son. And the trail boss followed him from the hall.

Balance remained himself only a few minutes longer. He could not see that anything good was going to come out of this meeting— the real damage had been done with the reinstating of the police force. He went out and down the steps, and at the foot of them Montgomery, the newspaperman, caught him up. The latter said, "I noticed you talking to Clayt Spearman . . ."

"It was personal," Balance replied curtly. "Nothing for the paper."

The other took that good-naturedly enough; he put away his pencil and notebook, took off his spectacles and mopped his face with a handkerchief. The evening was muggy, with no stir of air. A last gleam of lemon-yellow light stained the sky above the western horizon, matched by the glow of the rising moon. "This has really been a day!" the editor said. "I suppose you heard, the posse that went looking for Billy Thompson came back without raising sign of him."

Balance nodded. "I don't imagine they looked too hard!"

"Somebody else that seems to have left for parts unknown is that fellow John Sterling. I've been looking for him, to get a statement, and nobody's seen the man. He had a horse at the livery, and it's gone—Nagle says he sneaked it out without paying his bill. I imagine Ellsworth has seen the last of him."

"Why should he stay—just to face Ben Thompson again," Balance agreed. "The whole affair began with him." He added: "What's the news of Whitney?"

"Not good," the sheriff's brother-in-law admitted. "He's suffering pretty fierce—nothing either of our local doctors seem able to do. I've wired the post surgeon at Fort Riley."

Balance was struck by a thought. "The best man I know with gun-shot wounds is Howard Radley, at Abilene. I've heard him speak well of Cap Whitney. I know if he was asked, he'd be glad to help any way he could."

"Why, thanks," Montgomery said. "That's an excellent suggestion. I'll get off a wire, directly . . ."

In the aftermath of such a day the night seemed subdued, un-usually quiet. Balance got a stogie to burning and walked across the plaza to the Oriental Palace. Business there was slow. He asked the bartender on duty if Joe Glennon was in his office and got a shake of head in answer. Balance said, "I'll be back there if I'm needed for anything," and went on through the barroom.

The card rooms were dark, as he had known they would be—Ben Thompson was running no games tonight. Balance closed the bar-room door behind him, moved through the darkness to a bracket lamp on the wall beside the office entrance and snapped a match on his thumbnail. As he turned up the wick and settled the glass shade in place, he received—too late—the impression that he was not alone. His head came around sharply and he stared at the man who stood in the open door to one of the card rooms. The barrel of a rifle glinted in the lamplight, the muzzle trained at his chest.

Billy Thompson said hoarsely, "Well, don't stand there! Come in and bring the lamp with you . . ."

Without comment, Vern Balance picked it from its holder; the other man stood aside for him as he carried the lamp into the room, freakish shadows swaying and flowing about him. The curtains, he saw, were drawn tight across the closed window; with the door shut the room was breathless and sweltering. Balance set the lamp on the table and Billy stepped past him and turned the wick down. His face, in the upward pour of light, shone with sweat.

"How long you been hiding here?" Balance demanded.

"I'm waiting for Ben," the other said, not really answering. "When the hell is he going to show up?"

Balance shook his head. "Wrong again, Billy," he said. "He told me he wouldn't be in tonight." And Billy cursed him foully.

"You're wasting your breath," Vern Balance pointed out, his eyes cold. "Swearing at me won't get you anything. If you're in trouble, you brought it on yourself." It was not a smart way to talk to Billy Thompson, especially with a rifle in his hands; but Balance was thoroughly out of sorts and weary of dealing with him.

Billy walked around the table, slumped into a chair and laid the rifle in front of him. He ran his hands across his face and through his tangled hair. Looking at him more closely, Balance decided the man wasn't drunk, but he was definitely hung over, unshaven and sick looking. Balance asked him coldly, "You had yourself anything to eat?"

"Sure," the other grunted shortly. "What you think, I been hiding out in a hole in the ground somewhere? Hell, I only went as far as Nauchville."

"I see." While the hapless group of possemen were out scouring the prairie for him, he no doubt had been comfortably holed up with some girl or other, whom he'd have had little trouble persuading to hide him in her crib.

Now Billy made an impatient gesture and placed both hands flat on the table as he peered balefully at the other man. "Look! I tell you, I got to see my brother. Do you know where he is, or don't you?"

Balance hesitated, saw no point in lying and nodded. "I suppose I do."

"Then for God's sake get him!" The red-shot eyes turned mean, and Billy slid a trembling hand to the rifle's breech. "Only, you damn well better not talk to anyone else while you're at it!"

"Take your hand off that gun," Balance told him curtly. "You've done enough shooting for one day. Cap Whitney was about the only good friend you had here. Do you realize you haven't even asked me whether he's still alive or not?"

Billy scowled at that, but a moment later he threw the question out. "Well—is he?"

"Just barely." Vern Balance turned to the door. With his hand on the knob he paused to say, "I'll fetch Ben. But you better watch yourself. I can't guarantee someone else might not happen back here, and stumble onto you."

"That'd be *their* hard luck, wouldn't it?" Billy retorted, showing his teeth. "So you just better hurry!"

Balance gave him a final stare that held all his dislike of the man. He went out and softly closed the door behind him.

At the Ellsworth Theater, the evening performance had already begun before the usual sell-out audience. A touring company from Kansas City was doing *She Stoops to Conquer;* the painted sets and costumes, and the spoken lines that came across the footlights, seemed oddly out of place against a fog of blue tobacco smoke, an occasional scrape of a spur rowel, the noisy interruptions of an audience who probably had only a dim idea of what the play was all about. Vern Balance moved along the aisles, studying the faces in the dim reflection of light from the stage, and presently discovered his man seated at the end of one of the crowded benches. He whispered his message and saw Ben Thompson's face show a reaction to this startling news. Without a word Thompson rose and together they left the theater.

Not to attract attention, when they arrived at the Oriental Palace they circled and entered by the alley door. Things were as Balance had left them, but they could hear Billy pacing—made nervous, likely enough, by his prolonged wait. Now the door to the card room was wrenched open and he looked out at them, and Balance said quickly, "I'll keep a lookout." Ben nodded and followed his brother into the room, closing the door after him. Balance was left alone in hallway darkness, hearing the hum of noise in the main room and, also, an occasional subdued snatch of talk beyond the panel at his elbow.

He made no effort to listen; he was merely anxious for the brothers to finish their business—in Billy's unpredictable moods, he couldn't be sure what might happen if Joe Glennon, or someone else, were to come back and find him. So he was relieved when finally the door was flung open. Ben came out first, saying over his shoulder, "I'm sure Whitney's going to be all right, but meanwhile you'd best to get as far from this town as you can."

"I got nothing to stay around here for," Billy muttered. He was carrying his rifle and was apparently ready to leave. "I'll look around, likely hitch on with an outfit heading back for Texas and trail south with them."

"All right." As an afterthought Ben said, "Here—you'll need this." He brought out a roll of money, peeled off several greenbacks which Billy took without comment and without thanks and shoved into a pocket. Balance was at the alley door, testing the night. He turned back to announce that the coast seemed clear.

Billy checked for himself, before he was satisfied; he slipped through the door and the night quickly swallowed him, and the other two listened as the sound of his boots faded. Closing the door, then, Vern Balance looked at Ben Thompson and could not hold back the thrust: "So you're still covering for him . . ."

Thompson looked at him sharply, in the dim glow from the lamp that burned beyond the nearby cardroom door. "What do you mean?"

"Telling him the sheriff will pull through—when you know Cap Whitney's dying! Were you trying to spare Billy's feelings? Do you really think he gives a damn, either way?"

For a cold moment he thought he had gone too far. The shadowed stare of the gunman seemed to bore into his flesh; then Ben Thompson shook his head and he said, in a voice that was almost too controlled: "Just stay out of my affairs, Balance. Do you mind?"

Vern Balance shrugged. "All right. He's *your* kin; I guess you'll do what you think you have to, to save his hide . . ." He could feel the other looking after him as he turned and walked out into the main room and left him there.

It was to be almost their last exchange of words.

CHAPTER XVI

Ellsworth had had an uneasy weekend.

Tension seemed almost a visible thing, like the curtains of heated air that trembled above the plaza. No one could have failed to see how many of those who passed beneath the awnings on either side of the tracks—Texans and townspeople alike—now wore their guns openly. The two groups avoided each other but the fact was there: Ellsworth was an armed camp, waiting for something but no one quite knew what—except that it had to do with the sparse reports that came, from time to time, from a frame house on the north side of town where a tortured man lay in agony, hovering between life and death.

Word was that Cap Whitney's lung had been punctured by the charge from Billy Thompson's shotgun, causing internal hemorrhaging. Now blood poisoning had set in and the sheriff's chances were being placed at near to hopeless. You just didn't survive a thing like that.

Vern Balance waited like the rest through this suspended time, observing, gauging, keeping his own counsel. At the Oriental Palace, his partner Joe Glennon grumbled and sweated and was visibly frightened. The card rooms remained empty; Ben Thompson kept to himself or to the company of his Texas cronies. It was a time when one thought he would almost have welcomed the punctuation of gunfire, as a release.

Monday morning Balance was in his room at the Drovers Cottage, giving his shoes a final polish for the day, when footsteps trampled through the corridor with a purpose that alerted him. He straightened, rag in hand, as a fist struck the door and almost at the same instant the knob was wrenched and the panel flung open, to rebound trembling off the wall. Before he could have made a move toward the gun beneath his coat, he saw a six-gun's muzzle pointed at him and thought better of it. He took his foot down from the seat of a chair and tossed the polishing rag aside, looking coldly at the intruders.

The man behind the gun was Norton, the ex-marshal, whose shirt-front still appeared to sag with the missing weight of the star that had been taken from him. His companion was the druggist, Ward Linker. Balance told them bluntly, "I didn't hear anyone invite you in."

"That's all right, Balance," Norton said, the gun unwavering. "Just keep your hands in sight, and what we come for won't take long."

"Watch him good, Marshal," Linker ordered the man, choosing to ignore the fact that he no longer carried the title. And then, as Balance stood motionless under the gun, Ward Linker proceeded to make a search of his room—the clothes press, the commode, the empty drawers of a bureau that he pulled out one by one; he even went down on hands and knees and peered under the bed.

As he got to his feet, a sour look of disappointment on him, Vern Balance said dryly, "Mind if I ask, now, what you thought you were looking for?"

The man threw it at him: "Guns! The word is, those Texas riff-raff have brought in a shipment of them. They plan to take over and burn Ellsworth to the ground; we aim to stop them by locating their cache before they have a chance to distribute it."

"And my room was on your list of places to search?" Incredulous, Vern Balance shook his head. "Linker, you can't believe this nonsense! A lot of things have been said lately, but it's been mostly heat and frustration doing the talking!"

Norton caught him up with a sharp warning: "Just watch those hands, Balance! I won't tell you again. We all know where *your* sympathies lie!"

Balance looked from one to the other, fighting his anger and trying to find some reasonable answer for them. At that moment a new step sounded beyond the open doorway and Jim Gore was speaking angrily as he strode into the room.

"Linker! By God, I'll put up with you in council meeting—but I won't have you throwing your weight around with the guests in my own hotel!"

Ward Linker swung to face him; the man's sallow cheeks were

stung with angry color. "This hotel of yours has always been a hotbed of Texan sentiment. I know what I have to do, and you can't stop me!"

"Oh, I think I can. You have no authority here. I don't see any search warrant."

"I can get one."

"Then go get it," the hotelowner snapped. "And don't bother to come back till you have!"

The two glared at each other, all the animosity of opposed viewpoints, of heated arguments over the council table, flaring between them in a silent duel that Ward Linker, finally, lost. The druggist sucked in his cheeks, and with an angry shake of his shoulders turned away. He grunted something at Norton; the latter gave Balance a last hard look and turned to follow.

Balance lowered the hands he had been holding well away from his body, under the eye of the ex-marshal's gun. But he wanted to make one more try with Linker, and he spoke as the man reached the doorway. "I give you my word: If there was any truth in these rumors that bother you, I'm positive I'd have known some hint of it. And I swear I've heard nothing at all . . ."

Ward Linker gave him no more than the briefest of looks, shot through with animosity. Then he was gone, taking the ex-lawman with him; as their steps faded down the corridor, Balance turned to Jim Gore and said gruffly, "What in the world's got into them?"

"Maybe you haven't heard," the hotelman said. "Whitney died this morning."

During a long stillness, Balance could find no answer. Slowly, then, he nodded. "I see . . . and this is the result. It's as though they held every Texan guilty!"

On a sudden decision Jim Gore stepped to look into the hallway, and then closed the door. Turning back he said quickly, "This is only a part of it." He looked dubiously at his guest. "You're really sure you haven't heard anything?"

"Well, I turned in early last night," Balance said. "And so far I haven't been out of the room."

"Well, *I've* been running around all morning, trying to find out exactly what's going on. You can imagine there's some that ain't anxious for me to know—me being too friendly with certain elements. But as near as I can piece it out, some of Ellsworth's leading citizens got together yesterday evening—while the sheriff was still alive. They formed themselves a vigilance committee."

Balance stared. "The hell they did!"

"Oh, yes! They've drawn up a list of undesirables—people they want rid of. Meaning Texans, of course. And some of those people have already been issued white slips warning them to leave."

"If I know Texans, that's only going to make them mad!"

But Gore answered: "I'll tell you someone who's already gone: your friend Ben Thompson."

"You can't be serious!"

"It's true. He left on the westbound, an hour ago. Not that I imagine they scared him any. I just think he'd had a bellyful of Ellsworth. Besides, Cad Pierce says that Ben as usual holds himself to blame for the harm his brother did.

"Anyway, he told Cad and Neil Kane he was going and advised them to do the same—said there was no good in this town any more, for any Texan. They didn't sound much as though they plan to follow his example.

"But what about you?" Jim Gore prodded, studying Balance's bleak expression. "If you don't look out, you just might find one of those notices slid under your own door." And he glanced there, almost as though he expected to see it lying on the worn carpet.

The other man said, "My conscience is clear. If I wouldn't run from Clayt Spearman, I'm damned if I let someone like Ward Linker give me my moving orders."

"Or—Happy Jack Morco?"

Balance made a face. "Not *him,* again?"

"He's bragging around now about being the one that *scared* Ben Thompson into leaving Ellsworth. If he should actually start believing it, he might get up nerve enough to go after some of his other enemies. I don't have to remind you, you and Clayt Spearman are high on the list."

"Now I'm really shaking!" Balance said with bitter sarcasm.

Belowstairs, in the hotel lobby and dining room, he heard talk to confirm Jim Gore's opinion about the seriousness of the latest turn of events. He remained aloof, however. He had a late hasty breakfast and then went alone to the Oriental Palace, through yet another searing morning's heat. But his thoughts were busy ones; and when he came upon a group of men gathered in front of Beebe's store, something in the way they fell silent as he neared made him give them a more careful scrutiny.

They were Ellsworth men—the storekeeper himself, a couple of others that he could remember shouting at him when he presumed to speak his mind in council meeting . . . and there was Ed Hogue. He walked through the stillness, feeling their stares follow him by.

But then some perverse instinct prompted him to turn back, to confront the new city marshal. It was as good a time as any to learn where the man stood, and Vern Balance fixed him with a look and said bluntly, "I'm wondering if you've got a piece of paper with my name on it."

Hogue was reputed to be a Frenchman; he had something of the appearance of one. He gave his questioner a scowling look. He said, "I ain't seen one—yet."

"All right," Balance said. "If you do, I'll be around. I'm generally not hard to find." There was cold defiance in the way he said it; temper had been running high in him ever since the invasion of his room at the Drovers Cottage, and Jim Gore's word about the vigilance committee. If the committee wanted dealings with him, he didn't intend to let them suppose he was afraid of them.

He deliberately turned his back, and walked on to enter the Oriental Palace.

There, sight of a man sitting alone at a table near the back pushed other thoughts from his mind. Howard Radley was filling his glass from a whiskey bottle; as Balance approached, the doctor stabbed him a look through gold-rimmed spectacles and nodded, then raised the glass with a hand that trembled slightly. He looked drained, and worn, his cheeks raddled with unshaven whiskers; his clothes appeared to have been slept in—at least, he had probably not had them off. His black medical bag stood on the table at his elbow.

He said, "I been waiting for you."

"Not too long, I hope," Balance said, and pulled a chair back for himself. Sitting, he watched the other drain off about half the shot, shudder a little, set the glass down. "I heard about Whitney. I guess you've had a bad time."

"Bad enough," the doctor agreed. "Even with three of us working. The way that shotgun took him, there was really nothing anybody could have done except try to ease the pain—and we couldn't even seem to do that. Damn it! He was too good a man to die that way!" Radley shuddered again; he shoved the cork into the bottle and set it aside. The whiskey seemed to have helped to calm nerves unstrung by sleeplessness and exacting labor and emotional ordeal.

"Well," Balance pointed out, "it's over now . . ."

The other man nodded dully, looking at his rope-veined hands that lay on the table in front of him. He seemed to stir himself, then, and brought his tired gaze to Balance's face. "So," he said, in a different tone. "You did come to Ellsworth. I thought you told me you were only going to stay overnight."

Balance felt a faint warmth in his cheeks, at the reminder. "It didn't quite work out that way," he admitted; and added, "Come to think of it, *you* said if I came here I'd end up killing someone."

"Well, and you're not out of the woods yet! I hear you just missed getting yourself lynched. I even hear Clayt Spearman put a price on you, and it was only thanks to Ben Thompson that no one's yet made a serious attempt to collect." He shook his head disapprovingly. "Stay with the world you've chosen, and you'll never be able to get away from violence."

"But it's not my choice, Doc. It's simply the only way I had of protecting an investment."

"Investment? You mean—this?" Howard Radley gave the barroom a cold survey. He shook his head. "When will you realize that likker and cards and killing go together? They always have—they always will."

"And you'll never leave off lecturing me!"

"Maybe I think you're worth taking the trouble. Though I ain't sure why!" The old man finished his drink, pushed his chair back. "Well," he said roughly, "me for a bed—and nobody better want me for anything until I've had a chance to sleep the clock around. And then—home, on the next train. Believe me, this town makes me appreciate the kind of place Abilene's finally turned into!"

Vern Balance sat and watched the doctor pick up his bottle and carry it to the bar, pay for what he had drunk, and then go out into the sunlight dragging on a broken-brimmed straw hat. For a long moment Balance stayed there, doing nothing—only half conscious of the desultory activity of the barroom as he thought again over his talk with the old man, more bothered by it than he liked to admit. Finally, with a shrug, he got out a stogie and fired it up, dropped the dead match into the sawdust and, rising, went back to Joe Glennon's office.

Alone there, he helped himself to Glennon's swivel chair and opened the ledger containing the current record of profits and expenses. He was becoming fairly adept at tracking the entries through the pages, in his partner's crabbed hand; despite a poor season, it was clear that the business hadn't done all that badly. In fact, except for Glennon's foolish extravagance in outfitting the new card rooms, by now the summer should have shown a good profit. And given a break, and a little more time, those rooms obviously would have earned out their cost and made a real profit for them.

But things had not worked out that way; now, because of the events of Friday, there would not be time. With Ben Thompson gone, who could they find to operate the gambling concession? Who had the know-how, let alone the reputation, to accomplish what Thompson had done for the Palace? Oh, no! Balance thought suddenly as an answer struck him. Not me! He slammed the ledger closed with a quick slap of his palm.

Unable to stay in one place for long, he stubbed out his stogie, dropped it into the brass spittoon, and picking his bowler from the desk, rose and went out through the building. He was so engrossed with his own restless thoughts that when he walked past the bar, and caught a few words dropped by one of a trio of trailhands leaning there over their drinks, they failed to register in his mind. A step farther, he suddenly halted and came around to interrupt the talk with a sharp question. "What was that?"

They looked at him, and the one who had been speaking blinked once. "What was what?"

"Rafter 7," Balance answered impatiently. "That's the Spearman herd. Did I hear you say it's gone?"

"It's supposed to be—just as soon as they could get it started and headed for Wichita. I was with one of the crew when word come to roust himself out to camp, pronto."

"And when was this?" Balance demanded.

"This morning early. Sounded like they hoped to be on the road by now."

A second puncher spoke up. "Somebody was telling me awhile ago, old Clayt Spearman has his ticket bought for the afternoon train to K.C. He's quittin' Ellsworth—and I know my own boss, for one, is all ready to follow him."

The first one, turning back to his whiskey, added to nobody in particular, "I got a hunch there may not be much left of this damn town when we do go! They got something coming—and these buildings should make a helluva bonfire . . ."

Next moment he let out a howl of pain as Vern Balance's hand dropped on his shoulder, hauling him around. Balance met his startled look with a scowl, but then he shrugged and pushed the fellow away from him. Rubbing his shoulder, the man looked into Balance's face and suddenly he was scared. "Not *me,* mister!" he exclaimed hoarsely. "It was just talk I've heard, that's all. I didn't mean—" But Balance had already turned on his heel and was savagely thrusting aside the batwing panels as he strode out of the Palace.

It might be no more than tough barroom talk, but he didn't like it. It fit with the rumors; and after all, the puncher was right—the wooden buildings of Ellsworth, crowding cheek-by-jowl and dried out to tinder by summer drought, would simply explode at the touch of a match.

He suddenly wanted very much to talk to someone about this, and it struck him that aside from Jim Gore—who, like himself, was tarred by being too closely associated with the Texas element—the one person he knew with a cool head and some degree of influence would be the newspaper editor, Montgomery. On an impulse he left his place beneath the awning of the Palace, and started across the plaza toward the frame building, next to the Grand Central, where the *Reporter* was written and edited and printed.

The door was locked, the green shades drawn against the day's heat. Balance rapped on the glass, and getting no response had to conclude that his man was elsewhere. He turned away in chagrin, and was going past the hotel again when someone called his name.

The Texans, Neil Kane and Cad Pierce, came out and Balance joined them beneath the ornate gallery, on the limestone walk. They had been drinking but they seemed sober enough, and angry. Pierce said gruffly, "How you like what's goin' on now?"

Balance told him, "I can't say I do. I don't like people breaking into my room without a search warrant, looking for guns that aren't there. On the other hand I don't think much of armed men parading the streets—or the threats I've heard about using a torch on Ellsworth."

The other quickly bridled. "It would serve them right! You think we should just tuck our tails and run when we're ordered to? Sure, Ben Thompson left—as I guess you've heard; but, with him it's different. Nobody in this town supposes for a minute that he's *afraid* of them!"

"And burning the town would prove the rest of you aren't?"

Pierce turned sullen, at that, and wouldn't answer. It was Neil Kane who said, "Yonder is one who's found the real way to punish this town!" And he nodded toward the depot, its roofline shimmering moltenly in the afternoon sun.

It was nearly time for the eastbound heading for Kansas City, and there was already activity on the station platform: people milling about, a hand truck being tooled out of the baggage room, the stationmaster in his billed cap and alpaca sleeve guards carrying a half-filled mail sack. Amidst all this—tall and straight, leaning on his cane with white hair shining—Clayt Spearman was an impressive figure. "You wait till all the rest of the drovers and owners start to follow Spearman's lead!" Kane predicted. "That should wake Ellsworth up, fast enough: Being left with nothing, just when it looks like there might finally be some action—and Wichita and the other towns ready to reap the harvest!"

Balance scarcely heard. His attention was all for the girl who stood at her father's side, dressed for traveling, her hand luggage on the splintered platform. She looked just as she had the day of the picnic; and Balance looked at her across the sun-struck open and shimmering rails and felt a pang of anguish, knowing that this was undoubtedly the last sight of her he would ever have.

Pierce and Kane were arguing. Only half listening, Balance gathered that the latter was of a mind to take the seven hundred head of longhorns he'd brought up from Austin and trail them down to Wichita—do it now, before too many others had the same idea. The suggestion angered Cad Pierce; it sounded too much like being scared out. Let the vigilantes serve him with one of their damned white affidavits, first.

"And *then* would you go?" Neil Kane prodded him.

"How the hell could I?" Pierce snapped back. "That would be admitting I was scared!"

"So either way, you're stuck—too damned stubborn to leave under any circumstances! Did you ever hear such reasoning?" Kane demanded, appealing to Vern Balance. The latter failed to answer. His stare was riveted to what was happening just then on the station platform.

He had no idea where Happy Jack Morco had come from. A moment ago there had been no sign of him; now he stood face to face with Clayt Spearman and, even at this distance, he could tell they were engaged in violent argument. All other activity on the platform had ceased; everyone there was staring and listening, making no effort to interfere. The angry voices came thinly, indistinctly, across the heated stillness. But when Balance looked at the girl, and clearly read her alarm and terror, he knew suddenly that he had to move.

Passing through the spindly row of saplings, he dropped down the dirt embankment and started walking quickly toward the depot. As he did so he heard a train's whistle run softly and mournfully across the Smoky Hill bottoms, somewhere west of town.

Spearman raised his voice in sudden fury, and his words carried to Balance: "If I stood up in council meeting and called you a murdering scum," he told Morco, "it's because that's what you are! No self-respecting town would have let you light, much less hung a badge on you."

The policeman said in a voice heavy with warning, "I told you before, I don't have to take that kind of talk from you, old man!"

"By God, it's the only kind you'll get! Now, leave me alone!"

Clayt Spearman added. "I got no more time to waste on you, *or* this town. There's a train I have to catch."

Tess had been tugging at her father's sleeve, trying to end this. The engine's whistle sounded again, blowing for the station, and now its bell was stroking. When Balance set his foot upon a rail it brought to him the rhythmic pound of drive wheels. He saw Clayt Spearman, giving to his daughter's urging, start to turn away from Morco.

"Don't show your back to me!" Happy Jack's hand fell on the old man's arm, gave it a yank that nearly flung him off his crippled legs. Vern Balance heard himself cry out, futilely. He saw Spearman catch himself, and the cane in his hand lifting—half threatening, half in a defensive gesture.

As though that had been what he was waiting for, Morco grabbed out his revolver. There was a moment of scuffling; the gun's barrel winked reflected sunlight as it chopped down, viciously. Pistol-whipped, the flat-crowned hat knocked from his head, Clayt Spearman started to fall; and even as he was dropping, Happy Jack Morco fired deliberately into his body.

The girl's scream mingled with the flat crack of the gun, that bounced echoes off the depot wall. Belatedly, Vern Balance remembered his own weapon; but even as he brought it out he knew he could not shoot, with so many bystanders caught in awkwardly frozen postures. Instead he shouted Morco's name; and Morco heard it, above the nearing thunder of the arriving train, and the clanging of its bell. His head jerked up. He saw Balance, standing in the cinders of the right-of-way. And with a convulsive movement of his whole body he swung the muzzle of his six-shooter around and fired.

It was a wild shot and the bullet missed widely. By that time, too furious for caution, Vern Balance was running straight toward the deputy. He still did not fire; but Morco seemed all at once unnerved. He looked at the man charging at him, and it was as though his entire face, under its rooster comb of stiff brown hair, crumpled and fell apart.

In the next breath he had whirled and, bowling a bystander out of his way, went running blindly off along the platform, leaving Tess Spearman standing dazed with shock beside her father's motionless body.

CHAPTER XVII

Vern Balance could not take time to learn how it was with Spearman. Not mounting the platform, he wheeled and ran along below it, in the cinders. Happy Jack Morco seemed to be a good runner. Boots thumping on the boards, stiff-arming men out of his way, he scampered the length of the platform and there took the drop to the ground, driven briefly to hands and knees but instantly springing up again. He cast a look back, to see his pursuer quickly cutting down the distance.

Balance thought he would swing left, seek cover below the edge of the platform; but apparently he thought the line of buildings near at hand along North Main offered better promise. Suddenly the eastbound was pounding into the station—bell ringing, brakes grabbing, black smoke belching from its diamond stack as the great engine filled the plaza with a punishing racket that drowned all other sounds. It was just what Morco wanted—Balance could almost see the thought hit him. Instantly he jerked about, flung up his gun for a shot that came close enough to make Balance break stride. And cutting sharply to the right, Happy Jack plunged straight across the tracks, his jack-knifing figure dwarfed by the iron monster bearing down on him.

He made it easily enough, but Balance was left with a hard decision. The train was slowing; to let it go by would mean an impossible delay, while it rolled to a grinding halt and blocked his path completely. Turned reckless by a determination to stop Morco for good, Balance ruled that out. He dug for speed, and hurled himself forward under the very nose of the engine.

The cowcatcher's iron scoop almost got him. He stumbled, went down in cinders at the edge of the rails as the throb of pulsing metal filled his head. Steam beat at him briefly. He wondered why he wasn't swept into the suction of the wheels that punished the rails so close beside him. But then he rolled to hands and knees and then to his feet, and found he still had his gun.

But where was Morco?

He supposed it had been imagination, not an actual gunshot he had heard just a moment ago, all but swallowed up in the noise of the train. He stood there close to the halted cars and peered at the line of buildings that faced him along North Main without seeing any trace of the man he was hunting. Grimly he started forward, because nothing was to be gained by standing here. Stubborn determination carried him. He knew he would never forget the heartrending sound of Tess Spearman's cry as she saw her father go down. This time, Morco had gone too far. He had to be stopped.

The trouble was, he *should* have been stopped, long ago—and could have been, even with the blind support of the council and the townspeople. It had come as no surprise to Vern Balance that the man was a coward at heart, as he'd proved when he broke and ran without Balance having so much as fired a shot. He could have been faced down and exposed at any time—the events leading to the death of Sheriff Whitney, and to Tess Spearman seeing her father shot down and bleeding at her feet, need never have happened.

Vern Balance blamed himself, and what he had considered a sensible wish to attend strictly to his own business. He should have foreseen that, in the long run, it would not be good enough . . .

He moved around a parked wagon and stepped up onto the boardwalk, holding the gun ready, admitting that he had no idea where to begin looking. And then he heard someone groan, and a scuff of shoe leather, and his head jerked and he saw the two men in front of Larkin's store. One was seated in a clumsy sprawl on the bench beneath the awning, clutching at his right leg that was dripping blood. Jim Miller, the town's mayor, was bending over him solicitously, as though trying to steady him there. The hurt man began to moan, on each intake of breath, each sound louder and more filled with pain and fright.

Vern Balance demanded sharply, "What happened?"

The mayor answered over his shoulder, "It was Morco! We thought we heard shooting, just as the train was pulling in, and when we came out he was running straight toward us. We called to ask what was the matter, and he"—Miller shook his head in disbelief—"and the man opened fire at us!"

The wounded man lifted his head and it was Ward Linker. The druggist's face was bone white and he had his eyes screwed tight shut; he was still groaning with each rapid intake of breath.

"Where's Morco now?" Balance demanded.

"He ran in there," Miller told him, indicating the entrance of the livery barn next door. And as Balance turned in that direction the mayor seemed to notice the gun in his fist. "You aren't going after him? He'll kill you! I tell you, I think he's gone crazy!"

Linker opened pain-filled eyes, to stare wildly at Balance and croak, "The sonofabitch *shot* me! Stop him! Don't let him get away!"

So now you know about Morco, Balance could have said . . .

The doors of the livery stood wide open, on a blackness that seemed cavernous by contrast with the shimmering light of the August day. Happy Jack could be waiting with his gun lined up for a shot at anyone who tried to follow him through the wide doorway, but Vern Balance refused to think of that. He approached cautiously, weapon ready, and then in a quick, sidelong step moved around the doorframe and dropped immediately to a crouch, his back against the rough wall.

Nothing—no bullet, or blast of muzzle flame. He stayed where he was a moment, testing the still darkness. From memory he knew the barn's general layout—the cubbyhole office in a forward corner, the stall area, the grain bins and harness racks and the section toward the rear where two or three rent vehicles were normally stored out of the weather. There would be a rear door, opening onto a small corral, but this he thought would be locked. In taking refuge here, Happy Jack Morco had put himself into a corner—not that driving him out would be an easy matter.

In one of the stalls a horse stomped and blew its breath into the manger; a mouse gnawed and scuttled somewhere in the feed loft. And now the eastbound rang its bell and was rolling into motion again, the very walls of the barn trembling as the massive drive wheels gathered power. Moments later the train was gone, and in its wake settled a stillness so profound that Balance, straightening cautiously, distinctly heard the popping of the bones in his knees. His eyes had adjusted so that the barn seemed dimly lit by the faint pencil-lines of daylight that marked cracks between the boards of its siding. Roweled by inactivity, he started forward across the straw litter underfoot, reached the stall at the near end of the center aisle, and paused there.

He had roused no response. He stood at the corner of the stall partition, his gun poked ahead of him, and breathing through his mouth in order not to cover other sounds. About half the stalls were empty at the moment; there were the small noises of animals feeding and moving about in their narrow confines. But Happy Jack Morco, wherever he was, had still made no move to betray himself.

Balance moved down the aisle, stepping lightly, gun ready for a quick swing in any direction.

He imagined he heard a slight noise, then, behind and to his left— like cloth scraping against a wooden partition. Taut nerves leaped; he started to whirl toward the sound, but in the next instant forgot it. For all at once a man's dark figure had erupted from a stall directly ahead of him. It lunged across the passageway and vanished into a cross aisle just beyond. And Balance saw it plain enough, in that frozen second of time, to recognize Happy Jack Morco. He gave a shout, and went after him.

The cross aisle led to an area where a pair of buggies and a buck-board were ranked against the barn's east wall. Here it was, appar-ently, that Happy Jack chose to make his stand. "Damn you!" he cried, in a voice that had the beginning of hysteria in it. "Don't come any closer. You hear me? It'll be the last step you ever take!"

Hesitating, his shoulder against a roof support, Balance tried to sort out the jumble of spoked wheels and tongues and wagonboxes yonder. It was hard to place a voice, amid the confusing echoes of the big building. The heat was breathless, cotton-thick. He rocked back the hammer of his gun and the sound seemed startlingly loud. "This has gone too far, Morco," he said. "You shot down Clayt Spearman with no reason, and no excuse. Someone's finally got to stop you—and it looks like it would have to be me."

"Try it, and you're a dead man!" Happy Jack almost screamed at him.

And then, just behind Vern Balance, a new voice spoke and the hairs stood up on the back of his neck. "Go right ahead, Balance!

You're a dead man, one way or the other. Because, if he doesn't get you—then I'll finish you, afterwards . . ."

He didn't have to look around, or see the gun pointed at his back. Too late, he knew now he should have paid attention to that warning sound of cloth scraping against wood. Caught between two guns, he said bitterly, to the man behind him, "You were supposed to be trailing a herd to Wichita."

"I'll catch up," Ernie Telford said coolly. "First, I had this business of my own to settle."

"Maybe you heard Ben Thompson has left Ellsworth. Maybe now you think it's safe to try to collect that five hundred. But there may not be anybody to collect it from—it depends on whether Spearman's dead, or only wounded."

"I ain't all that interested in head money," Telford assured him. "This is another matter."

Angie? Balance supposed he had to be referring to the night when he was prevented from mistreating the Nauchville woman. There was simply no other grounds he could think of, for a difference with the Rafter 7 trail boss.

And then he got the surprise of his life, as Ernie Telford continued; "After all, long as you're around to stir it up, I can't ever be sure when that business at Abilene might be reopened."

Vern Balance stiffened; he nearly turned, but checked himself. "And *you* want it kept closed? You, Telford? I've had two years to think about that shooting—but I could never find a way to tie you into it! I always assumed I was the one supposed to end up dead, not Bud Spearman. And you hardly even knew me . . ."

The voice of Happy Jack Morco came through the breathless stillness: "Balance! Why the hell are you stalling?" They neither paid him any attention.

Ernie Telford said, "You ain't got the picture at all. Wasn't no one supposed to end up dead at the table, that night. The game was only a way of setting you up to take the blame later on, when Bud was to be found shot from an alleyway—after publicly calling you a crook. Only, he turned out to be drunker and crazier than I thought; things got out of hand, but luckily you finished the job for me then and there. Saved me the trouble of killing him."

"But why should you want him dead?"

"Hell, you can't be *that* dense! With Clayt Spearman crippled, and his snot of a kid out of the way—who's been having things just about to suit himself, at Rafter 7?"

"Of course, it was you that killed Rand Harker and threw his body in the river, to keep him from telling his part in handling the cards for you that night. And now, you want to kill me . . ."

"Only if Happy Jack bungles the job. He's scared to death of you, Balance—but he deserves a chance!"

Almost as though in answer to his name, the killer in the shadows yonder called again: "Damn you, Balance! *Where are you?*"

The voice in Vern Balance's ear said, "Go get it over with!" And without a warning a hand struck his shoulder and propelled him forward, into the open.

He tried to catch his footing, then instead let himself go down; in the moment of falling that gun in front of him went off and the fire from its muzzle seared his vision. The sound of the explosion beat deafeningly in the enclosed space, but the bullet was high and Balance dropped into the floor litter, landing heavily on left shoulder and elbow.

Instinct kept him moving, and reason told him his one faint advantage could be in not doing what was expected. Ernie Telford would be holding off, intending to let the other two fight this out. Balance rolled over onto his back and with dazzled vision hunted for Telford, thought he made out the roof support beside which the trail boss must be standing. He fired, more or less blindly, and thumbed back the hammer.

Telford must have been startled, for he was slow to respond and then too hasty for accuracy. At the roar of the gun something hit Balance a blow in the upper arm but he felt it scarcely as pain. Elbow braced against the floorboards, he threw a shot directly above and to the left of the smear of flame. And at once he was rolling once more, belly down, as Happy Jack Morco reared up from his hiding place.

The deputy made a black shape, towering above the one who lay prone with elbows braced and gun held steady in both hands; both men fired, in almost the same instant. There was a punishing wallop of sound. The shadow of Morco was suddenly wiped away from in front of Balance, as the deputy was flung bodily around to smash against the tall, spindly wheel of a surrey. And then it was all over, and Balance lay stunned by violence, and with powdersmoke swirling about him.

Caution brought him to his feet, shaking more than a little as he looked about him for further danger. He was still holding the gun. He nearly lifted it when someone said, in an awed voice: "My God! Did you kill them both?"

It was Nagle's part-time hostler, a lean and stoop-shouldered man with whom Balance had done business a couple of times in the renting of a horse and rig. The door of the office, standing open, showed where he had appeared from. He turned away from staring at Ernie Telford's lifeless sprawl, and his stare fastened itself on the blood on Balance's shoulder. "You been hit!" Only now really aware of the hurt, Balance touched it with his fingers and winced; but at that moment it hardly seemed important.

He demanded sharply, "How much did you see of this?"

"All of it," the man told him. "I heard a commotion, and come out to learn what was going on. They had you boxed between 'em. I'll tell anybody that asks, you hadn't no choice."

Balance's hand shot out, to grab the man by a shoulder. "But what did you *hear?* Anything at all that was said, before the shooting started?"

The man blinked, and grimaced under the hard grip. "I wasn't close enough for that. I didn't hear nothing!"

"I see."

Disappointment, bitter and final, settled through Balance as he eased his grip and the man writhed free. For just a moment he had thought he saw a ray of hope.

Now as men began cautiously entering the barn, unable any longer to hold back their curiosity, he walked over and looked at Ernie Telford. The big trail boss was dead, right enough; he had finally revealed the truth, but the truth had died with him. Vern Balance faced the fact that there was no way left now, for him ever to prove what had really happened, the night of that other killing over a card table in Abilene . . .

CHAPTER XVIII

Joe Glennon was in a better mood than Balance could ever remember having seen him. He put down his pen, swung the swivel chair and patted the arms with his soft hands as he beamed up at his partner. "Good morning—good morning. How's that arm?"

Balance flexed it gingerly. "Better. Some painful, still, but it never was serious."

The fat man nodded, dismissing this—it seemed quite easy for him to be satisfied about someone else's discomfort. As Balance took a seat, Glennon turned back to the desk for a box of his expensive cigars. He offered one, selected another but instead of lighting it sat rolling it between the fingers of both hands.

Balance said dryly, "You seem in good spirits."

"And why not?" the other insisted. "Yesterday, I admit, I was scared—real scared. But that's all changed, of course. I suppose you heard about this morning's council meeting."

"*Another* one?"

"Well, certainly! When a town's been shook up the way this one has, they damn well got to make time. Two days ago they was ready to send for the state militia. Now they know it was no one's fault but their own, if they came within an ace of having Ellsworth burnt down around their ears. Had Spearman actually been killed by that crazy Morco, I doubt anything could have stopped it."

Balance said, "So what did happen this morning? Were you there?"

"I wouldn't have missed it! The council wiped the slate clean. They got rid of every last vestige of the old police force, and promised to find a new city marshal who'll be acceptable to the Texans. They all but apologized for the mess they made." Glennon smirked. "It's obvious what's got into them, of course: Now they've seen the light, they're scared to death the drovers *will* take their herds away from Ellsworth—just when all the signs are getting stronger that the market's finally about to pick up."

"You really think that's true, then?"

"About the market? Oh, it was bound to break!" Glennon bit off the end of his cigar, spat it into the cuspidor next to his elastic-sided shoe, shoved the cigar into his mouth. "No question about it," he said complacently, "we're about to reap the reward we've all been waiting for, this whole miserable summer. In another week or two the money should start rolling in!"

Vern Balance looked at his partner, seeing the same inflated optimism that had always been Glennon's fatal drawback as a businessman. He could feel no answering enthusiasm, and he said so bluntly: "I hope you're right. I'm not too convinced, myself; but since *you* are, this might be as good a time as any to discuss a deal . . . I want out."

The smile faded slightly around the cigar. The hand that was reaching to find a match paused in mid-gesture. "Out?"

"Out of the Palace," Balance explained. "And out of the partnership. I'm giving you a chance to take over my half."

Glennon was frowning, now. Balance could almost read the swift and puzzled thoughts working behind his eyes, as he deliberately took time to select a match and snap the head alight. He sucked fire into the cigar, studying Balance through the quick cloud of smoke.

"I don't understand," he said finally. "What's put this idea in your head, all of a sudden?"

"It's not all that sudden." Glennon didn't need to know just how long, in fact, the decision had been halfconsciously forming, or how the words of Howard Radley had brought it to a head: *Stay with the world you've chosen and you'll never see an end to violence* . . . Once, he had supposed that uncovering the full truth about the shooting of Bud Spearman would somehow ease his burden of guilt; but now that he knew the truth—knew how he had been used, a tool in a deliberate plot against the young man's life—he found it made little difference at all. Liquor and cards and killing go together, Radley had said; the rest was mere detail. But if he could not change the past and what had happened, the future at least was his to deal with.

He said gruffly, "It's my choice. Do you want to buy me out, or not? With business as promising as you tell me it is . . ."

But Glennon's expansive mood had been replaced by something else, in the instant that he saw how the wind was blowing. The fat man no longer smiled. He took the cigar from his mouth and looked at the glowing end of it, his lips pursed. And he said, in a cautious tone, "Of course, all that's in the future. Right now things are still tight as hell. You know how it's been, what with the amount we were forced to spend outfitting those card rooms—at your insistence, remember, and on your promise that Ben Thompson would stay to run the games . . ."

And the carpets? thought Balance to himself. And the drapes from Kansas City? The rich men's club in Chicago . . . But he let that go, saying merely, "What kind of deal *can* you make?"

Instead of answering, Glennon replaced his cigar and reached for the tin cash box. He flipped open the lid, removed a sheaf of bills and ran them under a thumb. "You can see, there's only a little over four hundred dollars here. And it's every cent of cash we have."

"Give me three hundred," Vern Balance told him, "and we'll call it quits."

Glennon was unable to hide his astonishment. "But it was three *thousand* you put in!"

Balance shrugged. "I want out," he repeated for a third time.

The cigar rolled furiously from one corner of the fat man's mouth to the other, as he continued to stare at Balance as though trying to fathom what dark plot might lie behind this madness. He said finally, "Will you sign a paper, relinquishing all claim to the establishment and to any further amount I might have owed you?"

Balance nodded. "Draw it up and I'll sign it," he said, and saw that, at last, Joe Glennon was forced to believe him.

Twenty minutes later he walked out of the Oriental Palace for the last time, taking with him a slim roll of bills and a sense of freedom—and, he was sure, leaving his former partner torn with doubt as to whether he knew some secret he wasn't revealing, or had simply taken leave of his senses.

Three hundred was not much, but it would do. It would take him away from here—whether east or west, it hardly mattered. Nor did he have any idea what he meant to do once he got there. A clean break was what he wanted, and a place where the past didn't need to follow him. He had nothing to detain him. His bill at the Drovers Cottage was paid, his carpetbag already packed; he would be traveling as light as he had arrived. As he climbed the stairs to his room, he felt free of more than the weight of gun and shoulder rig, lying once more at the bottom of the carpetbag.

No, he did not regret the three thousand. It was the least of his losses.

In his room he checked the contents of the bag and fastened it, and stood a long moment making sure he had forgotten nothing. Through the open window, all the familiar sounds of Ellsworth drifted up to him: a dog barking in the distance, a wagon creaking past, voices in the plaza below . . . He went out, then, closing the door carefully on a summer of his life; and he started along the corridor to the stairs.

The door of the room where Clayt Spearman lay, recovering from his clubbing and shooting by Happy Jack Morco, had been closed when he passed it earlier. Now it stood open, and Vern Balance hesitated, thinking it was only decent he should stop and pay his respects. But there was no sense in that. Even though his intervention had likely saved the old man's life for him, Spearman was not apt to have changed any of his attitudes. With a shake of the head Balance walked on past.

Beyond the open door a woman's voice had been speaking. She broke off, and now came Clayt Spearman's angry words, carrying through the stillness, and halted him in his tracks: "If you knew this about that Balance fellow, why have you kept your mouth shut?"

And the answer, in a voice he still didn't recognize: "I *couldn't* say anything, Mister Spearman—I was scared to death of Ernie Telford! He was a fearful man! One time when he had too much to drink, he fell to bragging how he managed things the night he got your boy killed. But after he sobered, he swore he'd kill me if I repeated so much as a word!

"Now that he's gone, things are different. I figured I ought to speak up."

There was a silence, and then the rancher said heavily, "With Ernie not here and able to deny it, how the hell am I supposed to know you're telling the truth?"

"Oh, Papa!" It was Tess Spearman, and the sound of her voice seemed to clamp hard on Balance's chest and impede his breathing. "Of course it's the truth! Can't you *tell?*"

No reply to that, for a long moment. When the old man spoke again it was to say, in a heavy tone, "I suppose she wants payment for this . . ."

"I don't want anything," the woman insisted quickly. "I'm only trying to set things right. I wasn't sure they'd even let me in the hotel, to see you; I guess I was *really* a fool to think you'd listen. But Mister Balance done me a real favor once. He—he treated me like a lady!"

And suddenly she came hurrying from the room. It was Angie, of course—the Nauchville woman. She had dressed in her tawdry best for the occasion, and she looked pale and drawn beneath her rouge. She saw Balance standing in the corridor, carpetbag in hand; her eyes searched his face, and then she ducked her head and was gone before he had a chance to speak.

Tess had come into the doorway; a hand raised against the jamb, she stood staring a moment at the unexpected sight of Balance, in the shadowed corridor. She had never, he thought, looked lovelier. And now she came to him, and touched his hand, and said, "Won't you come inside—please?"

He shrugged, and followed her.

The room was much like his own, the window shades pulled low to cut the glare of August sunlight. Clayt Spearman, on the bed with pillows piled behind him, showed the result of the treatment he had taken from Happy Jack Morco—his face, and his mustache, and the cloth that bound his head were all nearly the same color. But his brown eyes, peering at the newcomer, were as fierce as ever. "So!" he grunted finally. "I suppose you put the woman up to that?"

Vern Balance bridled at the charge. "I did not!" he retorted. "I had no idea Telford had said anything to her. I only learned the facts about the shooting, myself, when he bragged about it minutes before I had to kill him. I thought the secret had died with him."

The sharp eyes continued to bore into him. When the old man spoke again, it was with a grudging change of tone. "Well, you always claimed you'd never meant to kill my boy—but, was I supposed to take the word of some card sharp?" He went on before the other could answer: "Still, if the whole game was a frameup, I guess that has to put a different face on things."

He shook his head, his expression petulant. "Dammit, that Ernie Telford always was a mean sonofabitch—even if he was a fair trail boss and foreman. I used to think, now and then, I'd have to replace him eventually. Guess I should have thought harder! I got others in my crew with experience enough to do the job—and the rest of the men should sure as shooting get along with them better."

Tess had been looking from one to the other. Now she exclaimed, "Well, that's fine, Papa. But—what about Mister Balance? Through no fault of his, he spent two years in prison, simply for managing to defend himself. Is that fair? And yesterday—if it hadn't been for him—"

Balance said stiffly, "I certainly didn't come here looking for thanks!"

The old rancher wagged his bandaged head. "No, she's right. All those fools standing around that station platform—and except for you jumping in to drive that crazy Morco off of me before he could finish, I know I'd have wound up with something a lot worse than a cracked skull, and a bullet alongside my ribs."

"I'm glad that's all it came to. I'd have done as much for anybody."

Spearman agreed roughly, "I guess you had no particular reason to do *me* any favors!"

They fell silent. Balance felt uneasy, standing under that fierce inspection with his hat in one hand and the bag in the other. He shifted position, and Clayt Spearman said, "Looks as though you're leaving."

"I've decided to take an old man's advice."

"Dr. Radley?" Tess put in, and brought her his look of surprise. She explained: "We two talked about you, while he was looking after Papa."

"Oh, did you?" Spearman snapped. "And just what did the old goat have to say?"

She answered her father, but her eyes were on the younger man's face. "He said everyone had it wrong about Vern Balance, Papa. That maybe he never got off to much of a start, but that he had a lot of—the doctor said, 'promise' . . ." She colored faintly but she got the word out.

"I see." Heavy sarcasm was in the old man's voice; his stare ate at Balance like a corrosive acid. "And just where does this—*promising* young feller figure he's off to now?"

Coldly Balance retorted, "Even supposing I knew, I doubt if I'd tell you. I wouldn't want to take up any more of your time. I only—"

Spearman didn't let him finish. Breaking in he demanded, "How'd you like to take a run down to Wichita?"

Balance was left staring. "Wichita?" he repeated. "I don't follow you!"

"It's simple enough. I got a herd of longhorns headed that way, and a buyer from Chicago scheduled to meet me there and arrange a deal. It's obvious, laid up like this, *I* ain't going to make it. How about you going in my place—as my agent . . ."

"To sell your herd? I've never dealt in cattle!"

"Nothing to it!" The argument was dismissed with the wave of a hand. "I know the price I want; he knows how much he wants to give me. It's just a matter of seein' who can hold out the longest." Spearman's lips quirked in a bleak smile. "The way you stand up to *me,* you ought to have a knack for that kind of dealing!"

When Balance stumbled over an answer, the girl turned to him urgently. "He *means* it! Don't you see? In his own way, he's trying to make amends."

"I also," the old man snapped, "damn well need someone to sell those longhorns. You turn me down, and I don't rightly know who I can get."

"It's the craziest thing I ever heard of!" Vern Balance said slowly. "But if you're serious . . ."

"Where would a man get better training, than over a poker table? I'll tell you this much: You wangle me any kind of a price out of that fellow, and I got a friend with one of them Chicago commission houses that owes me a favor. I think I can interest him in talking to you—that is, if you think that kind of thing appeals to you."

"If you're serious," Balance repeated, "then so am I. I'm looking for a job. I'd like a chance to try my hand."

"Then why are you standing around? The sooner you get started for Wichita, the better!" The old cowman settled deeper into the bed, grimacing with the effort. "Myself, I'm beginning to think that old goat of a Howard Radley was right—about me needing all the sleep I can manage." He closed his eyes, immediately opened them again; he glowered as he saw that Balance had not moved from the place where he stood with hat and bag in hand, looking at the girl.

"Oh, hell!" Spearman told him. "If *that's* what you're worried about, she ain't going nowhere. She'll be here when you get back!"

And her swift, warm smile confirmed it.